# ROOKS AT DUSK

On the other side of despair, what is left to believe in?

**Chick Yuill**

instant
apostle

First published in Great Britain in 2017

Instant Apostle
The Barn
1 Watford House Lane
Watford
Herts
WD17 1BJ

British Library Cataloguing-in-Publication Data

A catalogue record for this book is available from the British Library

This book and all other Instant Apostle books are available from
Instant Apostle:

Website: www.instantapostle.com

E-mail: info@instantapostle.com

ISBN 978-1-909728-65-3

Printed in Great Britain

# Contents

# Prologue

The dark spectacle of rooks wheeling and dipping across the blue-black evening sky had always unsettled him, left him ill at ease, short-tempered, half-convinced that at any minute something very unpleasant might happen. Looking up and seeing hundreds of birds spinning and turning as one, like a rich dark velvet cloth being wafted and shaken across the heavens by an invisible hand, stirred a longing within him, too deep to be clearly articulated and too strong to be easily ignored. It was a longing for freedom, for flight, for faith... for anything that would raise him above the mundane and the ordinary and transform him from an awkward, stumbling individual into an elegant partner in the dance of life.

But then there was always the *noise* of the rooks – the terrible, grating, discordant cawing and screeching that invariably accompanied their magnificent patterns of flight. What perverse quirk of evolution, he wondered, had worked to produce such a hideous dissonance? Why did the perfect precision of their movement always have to be spoiled by the clamour of their song? It was an incongruity that felt to him more evil than accidental – like watching a ballet of the most exquisite perfection in which the orchestra in the pits insisted on playing out of tune and out of time, while the musicians simultaneously jeered and cursed at the graceful movements of the dancers on the stage.

Of course, he had often reasoned to himself as he grew older, that it was nothing more than the mismatch of sight and sound, unpleasant and disconcerting certainly, but devoid of any meaning or significance beyond itself. Yet still he found it impossible to break free from the little boy who'd sat by the window of his bedroom in his grandmother's cottage watching the birds flocking to roost for the night, irresistibly drawn by the choreography of their exquisite movement, but equally disturbed by the cacophony of their jarring music. Something had formed itself in his childhood consciousness that night; an irresolvable tension of meaning and absurdity, a struggle between good and evil, a vague but persistent sense that just behind the beauty pageant of the natural world lurked a horror show of long shadows and dark, unpalatable truths.

The tousle-haired ten-year-old boy in the cottage had stifled his disquiet by switching on the bedside lamp, climbing hurriedly into bed, and reaching for his dog-eared copy of *Treasure Island*. Soon he was losing himself in the pages of his frequently read favourite book before drifting into a troubled sleep. The fifty-year-old man driving out of the motorway services on a grey March afternoon in 2010 tried to clear his head of those all too familiar thoughts by getting back on to the M6 motorway, turning up the volume on the car radio, and heading south through the gloom to Manchester.

# One

## Coming Home

He was turning into his driveway just as the ten o'clock news headlines sounded from Radio Four. He'd been driving with the radio on since late afternoon, so he'd heard the same litany of impending financial crises and dreary political interviews several times over. Still, it was oddly comforting to hear the familiar voice of the newsreader confidently informing the nation of the things that were so important we all had to know about them. If someone in a studio somewhere was able to assess what mattered enough to be the subject of the national news, there must be some sense of order in a confusing world.

It occurred to him, not for the first time, that it would be nice if only there was someone who could do that for him – *do it on a personal level*. Someone who could remind him what really did matter, tell him what he should be really concerned about, explain why he felt much less certain about so many things than he once did. He sat for a moment or two, listening to the news headlines all over again and allowing the headlights of the car to light up the familiar scene in front of him – the neatly manicured lawn, the tidily trimmed shrubs, the bare skeleton of the now leafless sycamore tree in the corner, the house-name *Agape* inscribed on slate and set in the red-brick of the house just to the right of the front door. To a casual stranger walking past, it would have been indistinguishable from a hundred other semi-detached houses in the suburbs of south Manchester. But not to him. This was home and he was glad to be back there at the end of a long day.

He eased himself a little stiffly out of the comforting cocoon of the leather driver's seat, pushed the car door gently shut behind him, and hit the button on his remote key fob. The responsive click of the locking device gave him a reassuring sense of security. For a moment he stopped to breathe in the cool night air before he crunched his way across the gravel pathway and past the beech hedge to the front porch. Then, with an overwhelming sense of gratitude, he put down his bag, turned his key in the lock, pushed the door open, and walked in. He was home.

He knew this place and these people and, if he could be sure of anything in life, this was it – this house where they'd lived for more than twenty years, this hallway that always felt so warm and welcoming when you stepped into it, these familiar *things*. He loved the things that were part of home, things that brought into sharp focus moments that would otherwise have become hazy and forgotten, things that chronicled the passing of time and gave tangible expression to what made their life together uniquely theirs. He glanced around, taking it all in again, appreciating some of his favourites. The photograph on the telephone table of the three of them on the beach at Bude, trying desperately to look as if they were enjoying a

Mediterranean summer despite the icy cold wind blowing in from the sea on a dull June day; that always made him smile with an odd mixture of delight in the reliability of his family and despair at the unpredictability of the British weather. Or the piece of jagged quartz stone that took pride of place on the little rickety bookcase he'd inherited from his parents. They'd found that on a holiday in Arizona shortly after they were first married and brought it home as their only memento of the trip because they'd been too hard-up to buy anything decent from the souvenir shops they'd visited. And on the landing, halfway up the stairs, a poster-sized black and white photograph of Miles Davis, trumpet to his lips, which he'd insisted be hung there to celebrate his love of jazz in general and his admiration for jazz trumpet players in particular. They might be just *things* to others, but to him they'd become icons, embodying a significance far beyond their artistic merit or their financial value.

But especially he felt sure of this woman that he knew would be waiting for him. He and Jean had met at Glasgow University when they were both reading English more than thirty years before. You couldn't quite call it love at first sight, but from the very beginning he'd found her interesting, even fascinating. She wasn't one of the academic high-flyers. Definitely not one of the blue-stocking brigade destined for a first or headed for postgraduate studies. But she was smart in an uncomplicated, down-to-earth kind of way that made him unaccountably nervous whenever he offered an opinion in a tutorial. He always felt that she thought him pretentious and way too serious. Just as he was in the middle of some lengthy and opinionated speech on the merits or otherwise of a Shakespearian sonnet or a Victorian novel, she'd look across the room and raise her eyebrows in a way that sucked all the youthful bravado out of him and stopped him in his tracks. But then she'd smile disarmingly, and tell him to get on with it and make his point. And it wasn't many weeks into the first term before they discovered that they shared a commitment to the Christian faith and he began to realise that he wanted and needed her company and her affirmation more than anything else.

On their first date he'd taken her to a dull poetry reading in a dreary lecture room by a fellow student who was possessed of more enthusiasm than talent. They'd stayed for an hour – she always said it was the longest hour of her life – before making their escape and heading for the more convivial atmosphere of the college bar. And that was it, he always told people who asked how they'd got together. There hadn't ever been anyone else. It wasn't that he didn't share the same temptations as the rest of his sex, or that he'd never found anyone else attractive. It was just that Jean was so right for him, complemented him so perfectly, kept him sane and anchored. Why break his promises and spoil the best thing that had ever happened to him? He'd never found an answer to that question that would persuade him to cheat on her. Coming home was always good.

A voice from the kitchen roused him from his nostalgic reflections.

'Hello! Is that you, Ray?'

'Who else could it be?' he answered. 'Unless you've given some other a guy a key for the front door.'

'Well, I wasn't going to say anything. But since you mention it...'

Jean smiled as she came through to the hallway and they hugged each other just like they'd done a thousand times before. He recognised the perfume she was wearing as one she particularly liked and that she'd asked him to buy her for her birthday. If he'd been more romantic he would have remembered the name of it and impressed her with his attentiveness. But he settled for a simple, straightforward compliment.

'Hmm... you smell good,' he said. 'You must be wearing that just for me. I'm glad I decided to come home.'

'Yeah, right,' she replied. 'I've just been in the kitchen and I think I probably smell more of your supper than anything that might inspire you to be romantic.'

He stood back and sniffed theatrically, like a connoisseur with a nose for a good wine.

'Naah... it's definitely the aroma of the incredibly expensive stuff I bought for you. It *is* going to be a really good evening.'

He took a long look at his wife. She hadn't really changed much since those days at university. There were flashes of grey at the temples, but her short, wavy brown hair was as distinctive and attractive to him as it had been then. And, despite what she jokingly called 'laughter lines' around her mouth and eyes, her features were as mobile and lively as ever. *Attractive* wasn't just his description of her. It was the word that people who knew her most often used to describe her. She had a ready smile and an easy way of chatting, even to relative strangers, that drew people to her and put them immediately at ease. And he was glad he'd married her.

'Now you're talking a good game,' she said, kissing him again. 'But you look too tired for any of that stuff tonight. You look like you've had enough. I think you'd fall asleep before you could make the first move. What's the day been like?'

He was quiet for a moment or two as he threw his jacket over the banister and loosened his tie. His expression changed, and he looked up at her wearily as he sat on the stairs and took off his shoes.

'I *am* tired,' he said. 'It was the usual stuff you get at these conferences. I just seem to have heard it all before. And some of those guys are so unbelievably pompous and opinionated, so sure of everything. They've never had a moment's doubt in their lives. Or maybe they're just better liars than I am. To be honest, after a couple of hours of listening to it, it was a toss-up between atheism and Zen Buddhism! So I snuck off to a little coffee shop when I thought no one was looking and then slipped back in just before my bit. I don't think anybody even missed me.'

She sat beside him on the stairs.

'And how about your presentation? You spent a lot of time on that. How did it go over?'

'Oh, it was OK, I think. They didn't lynch me, and quite a few folk were complimentary about it afterwards. Somebody even said it was a prophetic word for the Church. Maybe it was, or maybe I just sounded as if I was ticked off by it all.'

He laughed as he said that, but there was more than a grain of truth in his remark. Ten years ago he would have described how he was feeling as 'a holy discontent'; now he acknowledged that he was just plain irritated by what had once been the source of so much joy in his life.

He'd 'come to faith' as a child. That was the terminology he used when introducing himself to a roomful of people at one of his seminars, but it wasn't how he would have described it back then, of course. He'd 'got saved' one Sunday as a seven-year-old in the old wooden mission hall – everybody knew it as 'the holy hut' – that stood at the end of the row of coal miners' houses where he'd been born and grown up. In his imagination he could still smell the smoky fumes and feel the glowing heat that came from the old cast-iron pot-bellied stove that stood in the top right-hand corner of the room and battled with limited success against the cold draughts of a Lanarkshire winter. And he could remember vividly the 'Decision Sunday' in Sunday school – an event that was held without fail four times a year when kids like him, whose feet could hardly reach the floor, were asked to be very quiet, warned about the dire consequences of unconfessed sin, and challenged to step forward and 'ask Jesus into their hearts' to forgive all the wrong things they'd ever done.

It had seemed the most natural thing in the world to do back then. He hadn't been tearful or emotional in the slightest. But he knew it was something that he had to do if he wanted to be good here and now and get to meet his grandpa in heaven when it was his turn to die – something he couldn't begin to imagine but that he hoped would be a very long way off. So, while the barely competent pianist played 'Jesus Loves Me' on the slightly out-of-tune piano, he'd slid off the long wooden bench where he sat with the other boys from his class, and made his way quite deliberately to the 'penitents' form', a rough wooden bench at the front of the room. As he walked up the aisle he could see the words emblazoned on the wall in front of him in impressive black-edged, gold gothic lettering: 'PARDON, PEACE & PURITY'. Though he'd never been sure what they meant or why they were there, they seemed to have a kind of mystic power so that he was always impressed, even a little scared by them. Maybe, he thought to himself, they contained some secret truth into which he'd be initiated after he'd made these first steps on the journey of faith.

His Auntie May was the Sunday school superintendent and she had knelt beside him and prayed with him. Her matronly black dress and thick black stockings gave the whole affair an air of gravity to his childish mind, and he imagined that this must be what it would feel like to stand in court in the presence of a stern judge. He'd repeated the prayer line by line after her, and confessed that he was a sinner in a matter-of-fact kind of way, though the only specific sin he could recall involved the theft of a blue model soldier from Woolworth's when the distracted assistant was picking change out of the till for a customer in a hurry. The entire transaction took only a few minutes, and when he walked back to his seat clutching the gilt-edged Promise Card that he'd just signed, he had the quiet satisfaction of someone who's been to the dentist, had the tooth removed, and found the experience to be much less traumatic than anticipated.

There was just a slight sense of disappointment that he hadn't felt something like a bolt of electricity shooting through his body, or that there hadn't been the kind of immediate and dramatic change in his life that he'd heard mentioned in countless sermons and testimonies. Since he was old enough to remember, he'd been listening to stories of drunks who were instantaneously transformed into models of sobriety, wife-beaters who became faithful husbands, and hardened sinners who changed into the gentlest of saints. In fact, as he would often recount wryly in later years, there was no evidence of any change in his behaviour at all. That very afternoon, on the way home, he'd punched another kid who'd teased him about a patch in the sleeve of his jacket, which had caused him to wonder at that moment if the effect of his youthful conversion had worn off almost immediately. But no matter: he was assured by a series of Sunday school teachers and youth workers over the years that 'a work of grace' had been done in his life that day and that Jesus was 'living in his heart'. That was a concept that confused him whenever he thought about it as a child, so he'd decided early on that it was easier to leave well alone, take it on trust, and not to try to work it out.

In some ways nothing much had changed for him since that time. He still felt like that seven-year-old boy, knew he was the same person, sensed the same awkward shyness in company, even if he'd learned to disguise it with the passing of time. He was still Ray Young, Eddie and Liz's son, Tommy and Mary's brother. Still spoke with the same husky voice and distinctive accent that immediately betrayed his West of Scotland upbringing to anyone with an ear for such things. Still felt deep down that being the smartest kid in the class didn't even come close to being good at football. Still loved discussion and debate. Still found it difficult to know when to back off in an argument. Still instinctively resorted to trying to be funny when he found himself in a situation where he could feel himself getting embarrassed.

But, for all that, those days were long ago and far away. The simple certainties of childhood and the unquestioning faith of his earlier years had slowly dissipated in the face of a growing tide of doubt. Not that he was ever afflicted by *self*-doubt. At least, not in the way *he* understood self-doubt. In truth, that was the one thing he was sure of – the fact that he was a distinctive self, a centre of consciousness, *a person*. He'd *always* been sure of that. He could vividly recall childhood moments that stood out in his memory as sharp and clear as frost on the windowpane on a winter's morning; moments when he'd find himself lying in the darkness and stillness of his bedroom repeating over and over again, 'I'm me. I know I'm me.' It was an overwhelming sense of *me-ness* as he described it to himself back then. But the stronger that sense of self, the greater the cold fear that seeped deep into his mind, threatening to engulf his being with the terrible possibility that there might be nothing else apart from his *'me-ness'*. What if it was all the product of his own consciousness? What if no one else and nothing else really existed?

If those moments were fleeting and could be quickly forgotten, at least temporarily, in all the happenings of childhood and in the rapid changes of adolescence, they nonetheless left him with a persistent sense of detachment from things. At one and the same time he could be totally involved in all that was happening and utterly convinced by all that he believed and experienced, and yet vaguely uncertain and questioning about everything. And in these last couple of years that questioning had come more and more to the fore. Over the years he'd built up something of a reputation as a passionate and persuasive preacher. There was no shortage of speaking engagements in his calendar, and when he stood before a congregation he felt alive on a totally different level, in the same way some people do when they're clinging to a rock face or riding a motorbike at speed on a dirt-track. The challenge of communicating truth engaged him in a way that nothing else did. Yet even while he was speaking with complete sincerity, there would be a part of him that was stood off just to the side, watching what was happening, questioning what it all meant, wondering, in fact, if any of it was really true.

'Are we going to sit on the stairs for the rest of the evening?'

Jean's words jolted him back into the moment.

'No, not unless you're going to bring my supper and serve it right here,' he said, getting up and heading towards the kitchen. The aroma of home-made leak and potato soup and freshly baked bread soon trumped the memories of childhood conversion and the muddle of youthful theological confusions.

'Now, that's worth coming home for,' he said as he drew up a chair and took a first mouthful.

'Any mail worth looking at?'

'I've put it on the tray with your supper. You can read it while you're eating. It's mostly just routine stuff – bills and circulars. But I've printed off an email that came for you from the BBC. They're asking if you'll do another early morning *Pause for Thought* on Radio Two. The vicar who should have been doing it has got laryngitis and has had to drop out. So they're wondering if you can get four or five ready to record the day after tomorrow. And there's a text from our very own Ollie saying his Edinburgh gig is going OK, though it isn't paying as well as he hoped.'

He grimaced at the sound of the name 'Ollie'. Jean passed him her phone and he read the message from his only son with a rueful smile:

> Greetings, aged and venerable parents. I'm suffering for my art. Gigs are going well, digs are fine – no rats this time – but they're not paying me anything like my comic genius deserves. Still, I'm warding off starvation and managing to fight off the thousands of devoted fans who just want to meet me and sit at my feet. (Yeah, right!) See you before too long. Ollie.

Ray had often teased his son about the social and spiritual decline in the status of the family in just one generation: father becomes a respected church leader and conference speaker, son plumps for a career as a stand-up comic with a stage name that drives his dad crazy! As to whether that progression was down to the leadings of divine guidance, the result of relentless fate, or merely the vagaries of mindless fortune, he was less and less sure. But resolving that conundrum and responding to the BBC was work for tomorrow. Tonight he was just too hungry and too tired.

# Two

## The God-slot

It was just beginning to rain lightly when Ray parked his car in a side street and walked the short distance up the hill to the tram station at Timperley. The morning rush hour had cleared and the platform was deserted apart from two giggling teenage girls who were oblivious to the drizzle and who, he thought, should have been at school, and a much more serious-looking elderly couple sharing an old black umbrella, who looked as if they might have just heard some bad news.

His earlier years spent pastoring local churches had given him an instinct for such troubled people, and it briefly occurred to him that he should approach them and ask if they were all right. But before he could act on the impulse, the tram arrived and he reasoned it would be inappropriate to intrude on their apparent misfortune sitting in the tram where they might be overheard. As he settled into a seat, he acknowledged to himself that he was more than a little relieved that his by now somewhat rusty pastoral skills had not been called into play. He'd become much more comfortable talking to groups or even preaching to large congregations than speaking one-on-

one with individuals. It was easier to declaim objective truths from a pulpit, he'd discovered over the years, than to get involved in the messy details of people's lives. The neat answers of his well-crafted sermons didn't always work so well in the awkward moral dilemmas and emotional dissonances of everyday situations.

By the time the tram had pulled into St Peter's Square, the light drizzle had become a steady downpour, so he sheltered momentarily on the platform before summoning up his courage and heading towards Oxford Road and the BBC studios. After just a couple of hundred yards, he was already regretting the fact that he'd forgotten to pick up his umbrella when he left home. He and Jean had lived in Manchester for a quarter of a century and he was always ready to defend his adopted city against the criticisms of those who insisted that it was the wettest place in England. But this morning he had to admit that the weather looked as if it had set in and that a thoroughly unpleasant day was in prospect. By the time he reached his destination he was wet and miserable and wishing he'd never left home.

The receptionist at the BBC knew him from his previous visits and greeted him cheerily as he came through the sliding doors.

'Hi, Ray. You look like a drowned rat. Haven't you got an umbrella?'

He managed to force a smile as he wiped his head with a handkerchief and shook the rain off his clothes. But the man at the desk was already picking up the phone.

'You're here to record the night-time God-slot for Radio Two. They're expecting you. I'll give 'em a buzz. Someone will be down in five minutes to take you to the studio.'

He acknowledged the receptionist's comments, hoping he sounded more agreeable than he felt, and settled into one of the comfortable red chairs in the foyer. At least he could use the time to read through his double-spaced neatly typed scripts one more time. The email asking him at such short notice to cover for another contributor who'd gone down with laryngitis hadn't put him under any pressure. Having been involved with religious broadcasting for more than two decades, he figured he knew the technique well enough to get something down on paper and ready for recording at the drop of a hat.

He'd learned over the years that the only way to sound natural and conversational on the radio in a ninety-second spot – especially one that went out in the early hours of the morning – was to write it out verbatim, eliminating every unnecessary word and phrase. The formula was tried and tested: keep your language down to earth, avoid religious jargon, comment briefly on some item on the news or some incident from everyday life, throw in a touch of humour if possible, and then draw it to a conclusion with some kind of 'spiritual' application without being too heavy. The trouble was that the better he got at doing it – and producers often told him he was pretty good – the more dissatisfied he became. It was that spiritual twist at the end, the neat and tidy moralising that irritated him more and more. He would sometimes parody it in his head as he was driving along on his own with a cynical chuckle:

> And as I drive past this scrapyard I can't help but think to myself, isn't life like that – people on the scrap heap of life. But then I remember that they too can be recycled…

Of course, he was too practised at it to be as clumsy as that, but he felt that it was too close to the reality of what he was doing for comfort.

The trouble was that it served to highlight the problem that was gnawing away at his mind. He hadn't suddenly stopped believing the things he'd believed for years, even the stuff he'd been taught as a kid. None of that really bothered him. He could still put up a cogent argument and make a rational defence of faith in general and his Christian beliefs in particular. He didn't even have a problem with the miracle stories in the Gospels or the bold claim that 2,000 years ago an itinerant rabbi had been crucified and buried and then raised from the dead. It wasn't those things that were getting to him. It was just that, like the spiritual punchline to his God-spots on the radio, his faith was becoming an add-on, something to be shoehorned into the normal business of life, something that neither convinced him emotionally nor connected to the reality of his everyday life any longer.

'You must be Ray Young. I'm Annie Chaplin.'

He looked up into the face of a woman in her mid to late thirties. Her short blonde hair was streaked with highlights, and her smile was half-quizzical, half-amused as if she'd just made a joke and was waiting for a response. As he stood up and reached out to shake her hand, she spoke again before he could reply.

'I've just taken over producing this spot. We haven't met, but I googled you and found a photo. So I knew who to look for.'

'Well, you've got the advantage over me,' he replied, not quite sure why he felt slightly embarrassed by their encounter or why his words seemed to be not quite the right response. 'But it's good to meet you,' he added quickly, hoping she hadn't noticed his slight hesitancy.

'Likewise,' she said. 'Let me take you up to the studio.'

They walked through the turnstile barrier and got into the waiting lift. Ray was relieved when the doors opened onto the first floor after less than a minute. Over the years he'd mastered the art of casual conversation with strangers, but making small talk in a confined space with damp clothes and wet hair, and with a young woman who already seemed to have his measure felt particularly awkward on this morning. It was good to get into the studio with its familiar array of recording equipment and to lay out his A4 typed sheets on the desk in front of him. Immediately he relaxed as he glanced at his carefully prepared scripts; these were *his* thoughts, *his* words and, for at least the next few minutes, *he* was in control. He went through his usual routine of settling himself in his chair and clearing his throat. Then he nodded that he was ready to record, and after a couple of false starts to adjust the volume levels and eliminate an elusive electronic hum from a piece of faulty equipment, they got each of his five early morning spots done in one take. And that, he thought to himself, is that. Job done.

In years to come he would sometimes wonder to himself how things might have turned out if he'd just followed his normal routine at the end of the recording – if he'd politely declined her invitation to have coffee, just scooped up his papers, just slung his bag over his shoulder, just said thanks, just headed out of the studio, just walked back along the corridor to the lift, just stepped out onto the ground floor, just said a cheery goodbye to the man on reception, just swept through the front door, and just headed back to the tram station. It would certainly have made more immediate sense given the fact that his clothes were uncomfortably damp and that there was another appointment in his diary for that afternoon. And – just maybe – life would have followed its familiar course, and none of the events of the months that followed would ever have occurred.

What actually happened when Annie Chaplin asked him if he could spare half an hour to give her his advice about some ideas she was working on for a radio series, was that he looked at his watch, thought for a moment about his still damp and uncomfortable clothes, decided that he really needed to get home, and then – in spite of that conscious decision – heard himself saying, 'OK, but I'll just need to keep half an eye on the time and sit next to a radiator to dry off!' Which is why, just a few minutes later, he found himself sitting in the nearby coffee shop drinking a tall latte and listening to a woman he'd met less than an hour before talking about her ideas for a radio series.

'I got involved in religious broadcasting,' she explained, 'because of my own journey. My folks were never into church-going. Not that they were anti-religion or anything like that. It just wasn't on their radar. I don't ever remember us even talking about anything remotely religious. But my grandma had one of those old family Bibles, the kind where people used to record all the marriages and deaths, and it fascinated me. Whenever we went to visit her, I'd drag it down from the shelf and look at it. I was one of those kids who'd read anything they happened to pick up. And I loved words – the more archaic and strange they were and the less I actually understood their meaning, the better I liked them. So reading Grandma's Bible through the eyes of a child was like entering another dimension for me.'

She paused to allow a couple of people to push past and get to the table next to them by the window before launching into her story again.

'The rhythms and cadences of the Authorised Version just seemed to create a longing in me for something that I couldn't express and still can't fully articulate. Whatever it is, I'm still looking for it. I guess that's why I did philosophy and theology at university. Trying to work out what it's all about. After I graduated I did a stint at teaching, but when the opportunity came to get into religious broadcasting, I jumped at it. A chance to come at religion from the outside, I guess. I still don't have what you'd call a definite faith, though I have a real respect – even a degree of envy – for anyone who can make that kind of commitment.'

'So what's the programme you've got in mind?' Ray asked, glancing at his watch and wondering if he'd been wise to hang around in damp clothes when he'd another appointment in just over an hour's time. 'And how do you think I can help?' he added, his voice betraying just a hint of impatience.

'I'm sorry,' she laughed. 'People are always telling me that my enthusiasm carries me away. The point of telling you all this is that I'm fascinated by why some people believe and some people don't. I want to do a series in which I'd interview two people each week. One of them would be someone who has committed to a particular religious faith and the other would be someone who has lost faith and walked away from religion.'

She paused at this point, looked at him very intently, and spoke more slowly.

'I was interested in your stuff in the studio. I might have picked up the wrong signals, but I got the distinct impression that while you can tick all the right boxes and say all the right things, you're not quite as comfortable with what you believe as it might appear on the surface. So I just thought that you might be able to see things from both ends of the spectrum.'

He wanted to respond immediately with some kind of denial, but the words wouldn't come. Instead, he felt a tightness in his chest as a tear began to run slowly down his face. He wasn't sure why he was crying or what was happening to him, but he knew that there was nothing he could do to stop it at that moment. He was vaguely conscious of people at the nearby tables looking at him as the trickle of tears quickly became a torrent of sobs, and he heard himself mumble, 'Can we go now, please?' It was only when he reached the door and felt the cold damp air on his face that he realised that the strange noises he heard in his haste to escape must have been the scraping of chairs and tables on the floor as he pushed them out of the way. He was dimly aware of the traffic rushing past on Oxford Road but it felt distant from the reality he was experiencing right then.

Ray could never remember how he got there, but fifteen minutes later he was drinking a brandy sitting in an armchair in Annie Chaplin's tidy apartment while she looked at him with a mixture of bemusement and concern from the other side of the room.

'You feeling any better? Was it something I said?' she asked quietly.

'I think you just touched a raw nerve,' he answered with a wry smile. 'I wasn't even aware just how raw and tender it was.'

He gave a long sigh and then it was as if a dam had been breached. For the next half hour it poured out of him in an unstoppable flood – a bitter tirade of stuff long buried and suppressed that he'd never fully articulated or even acknowledged before: his struggles with a faith that had once been so simple and certain and now seemed so confusing and unsatisfying; his frustrations with a Church that had once been so relevant and now seemed so out of touch with everyday reality; his dissatisfaction with a life and ministry that had once been so fulfilling and now seemed so utterly pointless to him. By the time it began to subside he felt numb and empty and exhausted. And utterly unable to fathom why he had told all this to someone whom two hours ago he didn't even know existed.

Annie just stared at him: 'Wow! Where did all that come from?'

'I dunno,' he said sheepishly, 'but think it's time I went home. I'm sorry to have landed all this on you. I don't normally cry and complain to people I've just met.'

There was an uncomfortable silence as he stood up, uncertain as to how to say goodbye or how to take his leave.

Annie tried to ease the tension.

'Please don't be embarrassed. These things happen. And I would really love to talk to you again. Not just about the series, but about where you're at and what you're going to do about it.'

She took a step forward and gave him an affectionate hug. He knew he was blushing and he felt the tears welling up again. But he managed to mumble his thanks and add that he'd think about it as he drew himself away from her embrace. She opened the door and he hurried away without another word.

By the time he reached the bottom of the stairs and stepped out on to the street the rain had stopped and the sun was beginning to break through the clouds. He took a deep breath and turned towards the tram station. As he made his way through the lunchtime crowds he tried to make sense of what had just happened. Why had he allowed himself to behave like an emotional teenager with a total stranger? Was he having a breakdown? And why this sudden, crazy cocktail of sadness that was shaken up with something that felt like elation? It was too much to get his head around. But already one thing was beginning to force itself into his consciousness: he'd allowed something to surface that he'd been unwilling to acknowledge and it would be well-nigh impossible to put the genie back in the bottle. The events of the last couple of hours, he felt sure, represented some kind of watershed. But what it all meant and what the end result would be he had no idea.

# Three

## Stand-up

When the phone rang just before eleven o'clock on a Sunday morning in late August, Ollie Oldham was still fast asleep, having stumbled back to his Edinburgh digs around five o'clock after an exhausting day and an alcohol-fuelled night. Saturday had started unusually early for him with an interview for a lunchtime show on a local radio station where he'd recounted the story of how he'd survived his schooldays, dropped out of university in his second year, worked as a postman for eighteen months, and finally stumbled into a career in stand-up comedy. Normally he'd have grabbed a coffee and a sandwich after that and found somewhere to crash out for an hour or so before working on a new stand-up routine. But a chance meeting with a fellow comedian whom he hadn't seen in a couple of years had resulted in the kind of conversation that fills up all of the afternoon and spills over into the early part of the evening. Their reminiscences were brought to an end only by the realisation that it was time to head for the evening's gig.

As he mentally made some notes on the encounter – something he often did after any unexpected experience just to check for anything that could be mined for stand-up material – it occurred to him that 'filling' and 'spilling' were more than appropriate words to describe the nature of their meeting which took place in a cosy pub just off the Royal Mile and which was accompanied and facilitated by regular top-ups of the landlord's famed local brew.

The church hall just off Princes Street had been almost full with a more than usually enthusiastic audience for his one-man stand-up show 'OLLIE OLDHAM ON BIRTH, DEATH, AND THE OTHER BITS IN BETWEEN'. A group of junior doctors had enjoyed his perspective on life so much that they insisted he accompany them for a takeaway meal after the show. The night, they reminded him, was still young. Despite their pressing invitation, his first instinct had been to head straight to bed. But that thought was quickly superseded by the prospect of being treated to a spicy Indian curry and some liquid Scottish hospitality, and the anticipation that their tales of the more embarrassing side of medical practice might well provide him with some useful material for future comedy routines. He hadn't been disappointed in either of those hopes, his hosts proving generous both with their money and their anecdotes of life at the sharp end of the National Health Service. They'd even put him in a taxi in the early hours of the morning, though it hadn't required their years of medical training to realise that he was in no fit state to walk.

For the first few seconds the ringing of his mobile phone became just one more noise in the confusing dream he was having. Gradually, however, it summoned him into an unpleasant consciousness. It felt as if some malignant

32

being had managed to replace the lining of his throat with coarse sandpaper and to insert a small but highly effective pneumatic drill inside his skull. He tried unsuccessfully to sound as normal as possible when he eventually managed to speak.

'Hi, Ollie Oldham here. What can I do for you?'

The voice at the other end of the phone was a familiar one.

'It's your dad here, Ollie. So you can drop the Oldham nonsense. What on earth's wrong with you? You sound terrible.'

He groaned inwardly. The 'Oldham nonsense' wasn't a topic he wanted discuss with his dad even one more time, particularly when he felt like this. It was a fellow comic who'd suggested to him that Oliver Young didn't have the right resonance to it for the comedy circuit. They'd sat around one afternoon trying out various possibilities, none of which seemed right. Then he'd remembered that his dad used to call him 'young 'un', a nickname he'd hated as a kid.

'Listen,' he'd say in answer to his son's protests, 'you'll be an old 'un soon enough and you'll be wishing someone would call you "young 'un".'

Those reminiscences had started a train of thought which led to him to recall one of his earliest gigs in a working men's club in Oldham. It was a short leap from 'old 'un' to Oldham and the irresistible attraction of alliteration meant that it fitted perfectly with the shortened version of his first name. *Ollie Oldham* – that had a ring about it, he thought, which fitted perfectly with his comic persona as the cocky working-class boy who viewed life from the perspective of someone who's always on the lookout for the next dodgy scheme that will make his fortune. But it hadn't gone down well with his parents. It was hard enough for them to accept that their only son had embarked on the barely reputable career and totally unreliable life of a stand-up comic. The addition of a stage-name was, in their eyes, nothing more than an unnecessary affectation on the same level as having a tattoo on your neck or a piercing in your nose.

'OK, Dad,' he croaked. 'Let's not go there again. I'm all right, just had a late night. What's up?'

'Oh, nothing's up.'

Ollie thought the voice on the other end of the phone sounded just a little too casual.

'Just thought I might pop up to see you next week. Some folk I know in Edinburgh will put me up for a couple of nights. It's been a busy few months and I need a break. Mum's going to visit her sister in Bournemouth for a few days, so I thought I'd drive up on Monday and see your show. And we could have a bit of a chat. There's a couple of things I want to mention to you. Nothing to worry about, just some interesting changes on the horizon for me.'

The news that his father was willing to make a 400-mile round trip to see his son on stage was sufficient in itself to alert Ollie to the likelihood that this was something more than just parental pride. He knew his dad's turn of phrase well enough to suspect that a phrase like 'interesting changes' might herald some significant shift in direction. For as long as he could remember, his dad had been an itinerant speaker and church consultant, highly regarded and in frequent demand across the denominational spectrum. For many church leaders, he was the go-to person when they needed insight and guidance in the face of the powerful winds of change that were blowing against the fragile ship of institutional Christianity in the late twentieth and early twenty-first centuries.

Ollie's own gradual withdrawal from a traditional Christian faith and from church attendance had begun as a teenager and had hardened into rejection by his twenties. His mum had been more sympathetic and understanding, but for most of that time it had caused a breach in his relationship with his dad. In their occasional chats over the last couple of years, however, he'd begun to sense that his dad seemed a lot less sure about things then he once had been; he was certainly a lot less dogmatic. In his teenage years they'd locked horns frequently on matters of faith and morality and he'd always found his parents to be firmly entrenched in their convictions. Now conversations, apart from those that centred on his choice of stage-name, seemed to be a lot less stressful. He had a sudden urge to tell his dad that he loved him. But the words just wouldn't come. So all he said was, 'Sure, Dad. Just give me a buzz when you get here. It'll be good to talk.'

He quickly moved on to safer territory by raising a topic on which there had never been any tension between father and son. If faith and the Church had been the battleground on which their relationship had almost perished at times, football and the Theatre of Dreams had been the common ground on which they could always find enough agreement to allow them to co-exist throughout his rebellious teenage years. There had been long weeks and months when their shared commitment to Manchester

United had been the one thing on which they could see eye to eye. Ray himself often joked that his primary allegiances all began with the letter F – faith, family and football – though he confessed that he was never entirely sure about which order they came in. And Ollie was grateful that they had reached a point in their lives where they could agree on two of those things.

When the call ended, he pondered for a few minutes just what their upcoming conversation might involve. But he soon fell back into a deep sleep where he dreamed of being lifted up in his dad's arms surrounded by a shouting and gesticulating crowd. It was a dream he'd had many times in recent years and he could never figure out whether the other people in the dream were passionate football supporters inviting him to share their joy, or enthusiastic worshippers calling him back into the bosom of the Church. It was almost one o'clock in the afternoon before he stirred into life again and dragged himself out of bed and into the bathroom.

The shower in his digs was barely warm, but it helped him to shake himself awake even if he still felt hungover from the excesses of the previous evening. He hadn't left himself much time to get to the venue for the afternoon gig, so he was dressed, out of the door, and heading down the street within ten minutes of getting out of bed. It was a short walk to the pub where he was compering a line-up of young comics who were hoping that their five-minute spots would serve as an effective way of advertising and expanding the audience for their shows on the Fringe later in the day.

The sun was shining from a clear blue sky and there was a freshness in the air that showed the city at its best and quickly made him feel better. The animated conversations of the groups of people who passed him mingling with the sounds of the buskers who lined the streets conspired to produce a feeling of well-being that quickly began to verge on the euphoric. By the time he reached The Pipers' Kitchen and pushed open the door, he was thinking to himself that there was no place on earth he'd rather be at that moment than Edinburgh at Festival time.

Getting up on stage always had the same effect on him. It was the kind of exhilaration he imagined other people experienced when they climbed dangerously high mountains or skied down steep slopes. Practice helped, of course, but the element of risk was always there. Like everyone else in the profession he knew what it was like to bomb completely. He still carried the scars of the night early in his career when he'd been booked to provide the comedy at a charity boxing event in Liverpool. After the first bout the MC had worked the crowd up into an already raucous mood.

'Ladies and gentlemen, there's a generous donor here who's willing to give £1,000 to our charity if any man in the audience – yes, it's gotta be a man! – will volunteer to walk round the ring carrying the card with the round numbers – wearing only a polka dot bikini.'

The thunderous applause as he held the skimpy two-piece garment above his head went on for about half a minute before the fattest man in the room stepped forward, took the bikini and headed to the dressing rooms at the back of the hall. The ribald comments were still in full flow when the MC introduced the comedian for the evening.

'Now, here's Ollie Oldham. We've paid him good money so he'd better make you laugh!'

As soon as he got to his feet Ollie knew this wasn't going to end well. Already he could feel his heart thumping and the sweat begin to pour from his body. His material in those early days was built around stories of his slight dyslexia and the scrapes it had got him into. From the vantage point of hindsight it was obvious that it wasn't the most appropriate stuff for a working-class audience, but at that stage in his career he didn't have too many routines to choose from. He briefly thought of switching to the one that featured stories about football crowds, but he knew that would be tantamount to suicide for a Manchester lad in a Liverpool venue. An uphill task quickly became mission impossible. He'd just got to the one-liner in which he explained that dyslexia wasn't nearly so bad now that he was old enough to 'walk into a bra' when the mic cut out. The man sitting in front of the sound desk asked for the mic and Ollie passed it to him, assuming that he was going to replace the fading battery. His assumption was correct. But he wasn't ready for what happened next.

Before handing it back to him, the sound technician tapped it with his finger to ensure it was working and then yelled through the mic in a strong Scouse accent, 'You're garbage, mate!' The raucous roars of the crowd signalled all too clearly that they were in full agreement. The next five minutes passed in a blur. He was so relieved to get off in one piece that without stopping to ask for his cheque, he got straight into the borrowed twelve-year-old Mini he was driving and drove home as fast as he could.

But now he was almost grateful for that kind of experience. It reminded him of those painful accidents when he was learning to ride a bike, when his dad would pick him up, wipe his tears and tell him that you couldn't be a real cyclist until you'd fallen off a few times. It was an adage that held true as much for stand-up comedy as bike-riding. The act of balancing was all the more liberating because you remembered that it was a hard-won skill and one that might desert you in a moment if you gave into overconfidence or took it for granted. And this afternoon he was feeling all the freedom of the ride as he stepped up to the mic to do his ten-minute spot before introducing the other four young comedians who were waiting somewhat nervously off to the side of the stage. This was an audience that combined a thirst for an afternoon pint with an appetite for an hour of comedy and he knew very well how to handle them. He took the mic from the stand and wandered over to the bar looking for the person most likely to provide some comic opportunity.

'Good afternoon. I'm Ollie Oldham and this is Comedy Hour at The Pipers' Kitchen. And I'm just gonna say hello to one or two of these reprobates over at the bar.'

He knew he'd struck lucky when he spotted an overweight middle-aged man wearing a burgundy blazer with black and yellow stripes that would have looked more at home in the members' enclosure at Wimbledon than in an Edinburgh pub. The sight of the cravat tucked into the man's smart white shirt left Ollie in no doubt that he wasn't a regular at this particular drinking hole. He greeted his victim with an overexuberant pat on the back and asked him where he was from.

'I'm from Surrey,' he replied. The received pronunciation in which the words were delivered brought some ironic cheers.

'And what's your name?'

'Well, actually, it's Montague.'

That was too good an opportunity to miss. He had a one-liner ready for just such a moment.

'And is that your real name, or are you on the run from the police?'

When the laughter subsided, the man in the blazer assured his interviewer that it was indeed the name on his birth certificate, but that his friends called him Monty and he could do the same.

'Well, thank you, Monty,' Ollie retorted mimicking his public school accent as he repeated his name. 'You're welcome. Just a word of advice. Be careful. Dressed like that you look like one of the only half dozen Tories left in Scotland. The natives up here are not always sympathetic to you boys. But if you buy them a drink, you might just get out alive.'

A little more interrogation led to the revelation that the English visitor had been up early in the morning to explore the streets of the old city, having fortified himself with a hearty Scottish fry-up. And that was the cue Ollie needed to allow him to launch into a routine on the subject of his dislike of mornings and 'morning people'. It was obvious from the reaction that the men in his audience shared his aversion to those hours between six and ten in the morning. He didn't actually have a girlfriend just at that time, but his comic persona meant that, whatever his real-life situation in relation to the opposite sex, there always had to be a woman in his life. In this case, she was a woman who loved mornings, a woman who insisted on pulling back the curtains, allowing the light to disturb Ollie's slumbers, a woman who even had an evil morning gun – though she insisted on calling it a hairdryer – with which to shatter the peace of the quietest daybreak. He riffed on this theme for another few minutes – drawing grunts of approval from the men in the audience and mild but good-natured protests from their female companions – before introducing the first of the hopeful young comics on the bill.

'Get more spontaneous laughs, use less of your prepared material' was the maxim he'd been given by an old pro in his early stand-up career. So he'd learned the importance of gauging the response of his audience and watching for anyone who might provide ready fodder for some off-the-cuff banter. That's why he spotted the two women sat in the corner as he was leaving the small stage opposite the bar. The older of the two, who would have been in her late forties, he guessed, was sipping a glass of red wine. Her companion, a young woman in her early twenties, dressed in skinny jeans and a loose green top, with fair skin, sparkling green eyes, and a shock of shoulder-length, copper-coloured hair, was drinking a cup of tea – certainly not the usual tipple in a Scottish pub, even at lunchtime. For all that, she was laughing readily and seemed to be enjoying his routine. In fact, she seemed to be attracting the attention of people sat in that part of the room with her infectious laughter and striking appearance.

As he headed for the gents, Ollie thought to himself that he'd dialogue with her when he introduced the next act. She'd be easy to spot even though the pub was steadily filling up and becoming quite crowded, and she looked as if she'd know how to respond. But when he came back into the pub a couple of minutes later and scanned the room, it was to discover that the girl with the flowing copper-coloured hair was no longer there. Of course, he knew that with lunchtime audiences people were constantly coming and going, so he quickly changed tack, found another unsuspecting victim to pick on, and got on with the show. But he was disappointed that she'd gone and he resolved to ask around in case anyone knew her. An attractive red-head with good dress sense and the courage to drink tea in an Edinburgh pub had to be interesting, especially to an eligible young bachelor with no current girlfriend.

# Four

## Father and Son

It was just before ten o'clock on Wednesday morning and Ollie was generally in good spirits. As he sauntered along the cobbled surface of the Royal Mile he listed to himself the things that were contributing to his feeling of well-being: last night's gig had gone well; the *Edinburgh Evening News* had printed an enthusiastic review of his show – 'Ollie Oldham's one to look out for, a young man with a big future in comedy' was the bit he liked best; the sun was shining, and for the second day in succession there seemed little prospect of rain – something he'd learned never to take for granted in Scotland's capital city; and knowing that he was meeting his dad for breakfast he'd gone straight back to his digs and got to bed before midnight. It was the first morning in his two weeks in Edinburgh when he hadn't started the day with a hangover, and he acknowledged ruefully that it did make the morning not only bearable but almost pleasant.

The only cloud on the otherwise clear blue sky of the day ahead was his niggling concern as to why his dad had driven from Manchester just to talk to him about 'some interesting changes'. He had pretty well rejected the fixed faith and strict standards of his upbringing, but the fact that his parents remained firm in their beliefs and lifestyle provided an anchor point and a stability that he found comforting as he negotiated his route through an uncertain world and an unpredictable career. He thought of their religious convictions as being a bit like the castle that loomed over the entire city and stood just at the end of the street on which he was walking: it might not be relevant to his life in the twenty-first century and he'd no great interest in stumping up the admission fee to visit the ancient monument, but it was good to know that it was there all the same. It was a reminder of the past, and a focus for tall tales and magical myths that contained just enough historical truth and sufficient moral teaching to ensure that it remained a significant if minority interest in a very different world.

Even that small cloud quickly lifted, however, as he pushed open the door of the imaginatively named 'Prince Charlie's Tipple' and surveyed what had become a familiar scene to him in the past couple of weeks. The ornate panelling and heavy flock wallpaper hung with pictures of the city in years long past; the natural gloom of dark-wood floors and furnishings illuminated by the glow of yellow light from well-placed suspended lamps, and the buzz of conversation from fellow diners and drinkers all combined to make this one of his favourite venues in the Old Town. It took just a moment for his eyes to adjust from the bright light of a sunny Edinburgh morning and allow him to spot his dad already sat at a table towards the far end of the room. Ray spoke first as they greeted each other with the kind of manly hug and back-slap to which they had graduated in the last couple of years after their mutual inability to indulge in any kind of affectionate physical contact during Ollie's years of teenage rebellion.

'Good to see you, son.'

'And you, too, Dad,' Ollie responded. 'Really good to see you.'

The unforced sincerity of his own words took him by surprise. He really was glad to see his dad and the obvious warmth of their meeting pleased him. He would have held the embrace a little longer but the older man eased him away and sat down again.

'Enough of this. The Edinburgh air is giving me an appetite. Let's have breakfast. And you can relax, I'm buying.'

Ollie grinned his thanks. He knew what he was going to choose, but he couldn't resist the opportunity to mimic his dad's Lanarkshire accent as he picked up the menu.

'I'm havin' the full Scottish breakfast: bacon, square sausage, haggis, mushrooms, beans, fried egg, potato scone, tomatoes and toast.'

Ray picked up his cue and in unison they both added the sentence that not only acknowledged the Scottish fondness for fried food, but also its possible negative impact on health. He'd taught it to Ollie years ago and the strange-sounding sentence had fascinated the little boy.

'That'll go roon yer hert like a hairy worm, Jimmy!'

They laughed with an ease that surprised both of them, father and son remembering the uncomplicated days of childhood when Ollie had doted on his dad's every word.

'An' I'll have the same, so I will,' Ray added, picking up good-naturedly on Ollie's Music Hall impersonation of a Scotsman.

The waiter, attracted by their noisy hilarity, came over from the bar to take their order. His face broke into a smile as he recognised his customer.

'Hey, Ollie Oldham! Saw your show the other night. Really enjoyed it.'

He pointed across the table and said, 'And this must be your agent, now you're reaching for the big time.'

Ollie laughed. 'No, he's my old man, Ray Young.'

The waiter shook Ray by the hand.

'Well, you should be proud of him, Mr Young. He's a funny boy.'

Ollie thought he saw a hint of pride in his dad's face as he gave their order.

'Thanks. Probably got his talent from me. But he's still broke and I'm still paying for breakfast. We'll both have the full Scottish.'

'Two full Scottish breakfasts it is. And what'll you both have to drink?'

Ollie had sampled several of their excellent single malt whiskies during his stay in the city and was sorely tempted to try another. But in deference to his dad's almost teetotal stance he decided that a pot of tea would be more appropriate for the company and the hour. That was enough to remind him of the young woman with the fair skin and the copper-coloured hair he'd seen drinking tea in the pub yesterday. Where had she gone? Would he ever see her again? Could his own choice of beverage act as a kind of sympathetic magic and bring her within his reach again? And what on earth was he doing thinking such ridiculous thoughts about someone he'd seen for only a few brief minutes and about whom he knew absolutely nothing? He turned his attention back to the moment.

They made small talk while they waited for their meal to arrive, but their exchanges had that awkward, stilted quality that always marks a conversation in which both parties are avoiding or at least delaying discussing the topic they really need to address. It was a relief when the waiter brought their breakfasts and they could limit their communication to brief comments on the joys of a Scottish fry-up between mouthfuls of food. By the time they'd cleared their plates and asked for an extra pot of tea each, Ollie could no longer ignore the feeling that this was likely to be the most significant conversation they'd had since the heated arguments that had surrounded his decision to drop out of university and follow a profession that caused his parents to fear for their son's future.

Ray drew his chair closer, put his elbows on the table, intertwined his fingers, rested his chin on the backs of his hands, and cleared his throat. Ollie recognised the routine. He'd seen it countless times since childhood when his dad was about to say something he considered to be of more than usual importance and he immediately picked up the signal, pulling his own chair closer and folding his arms.

'OK, Dad. You haven't travelled all this way and paid for breakfast just to ask how I'm doing. What's this all about?'

Ray took a deep breath and let out a long, slow sigh.

'Well… you might have picked up that I've been a bit unsettled lately. I don't know whether it's some kind of delayed mid-life crisis or what it is. I just don't want to do the stuff I've been doing for so many years. And an opportunity's come up in the last couple of months that I think I want to follow through on.'

Ollie realised that he was feeling more than a little nervous at what his dad might be about to reveal. So he did what he'd always done in tense situations for as long as he could remember. He tried to make a joke.

'Don't tell me that they've asked you on to the coaching staff at Old Trafford. I mean, they must be aware of your expert opinions after all the years you've shouted your advice from the stands.'

'If only!' Ray laughed. 'Naah, be serious for once!'

Ray tried to sound casual, but a nervous cough signalled his uncertainty about what he was about to say and how his son might respond to it.

'What happened is that I met a really interesting religious affairs producer at the BBC a few months ago who asked me for some help with a project. I was a bit reluctant at first, but I've got more and more into it as the time's gone on. We've already done a fair bit of work together, looking at what makes some people commit to faith and why some of those same people reach a point in their lives where they don't or can't believe any longer. If I'm honest, I'm at a place a bit like that myself at the moment. I haven't suddenly become a disciple of Richard Dawkins or any of those crazy guys. I'm just struggling to see the point of it all. The other Sunday I was in the middle of a sermon and I suddenly realised that I was boring myself witless. The irony was that a dozen folk came up at the end of the service to tell me just how helpful it had been. That actually made it worse. Made me think that what I was doing was just some kind of performance.'

He paused while he poured himself another cup of tea. Ollie watched him with an overwhelming feeling of sympathy unlike anything he'd experienced before. It occurred to him that he'd never seen his dad look quite as tired or unsure of himself as he did at that moment. He wanted to say something helpful or encouraging, but he couldn't think of anything appropriate and he was relieved when his dad took up his story again.

'So I'm stepping out of public ministry – at least for a year or so until I work out where I'm really at and what I want to do – and I'm going to work full-time on the project. We think we might get a book out of it, maybe even a TV or radio series. There won't be much in the way of income at this stage. But I've got enough saved to see us through for six months or so. Thought it might be interesting to get your take on it.'

He looked at his son, waiting for his response. Ollie hesitated, pondering the implications of what he'd just heard. When he did reply his words were careful and considered.

'Well… I guess I'm surprised to some extent. You've been a preacher all my life and you've always seemed really secure in your faith, especially when I was an arrogant teenager trying to knock down everything you believed in. I can't imagine you doing anything different. I did think that I detected a change in you over the past couple of years, though I wasn't sure if that was just me becoming a little more sensitive and a little less cocky. But if it's what you want to do, then it's OK with me.'

He grinned at his dad and added: 'You've lived with me dropping out of university and doing stand-up, so I guess I'll cope with you stepping out of the pulpit and doing something else.'

They were both pleased that their meeting was going so well. But, as they looked at each other across the table, each of them harboured a deep and uncomfortable suspicion that it had all gone too smoothly, that the conversation hadn't properly ended, that the most important things had yet to be said. More in an effort to fill in the awkward silence than any real concern to solicit an answer, Ollie asked what he thought was an innocuous question.

'Who's the guy you're working with on this? How'd you get to know him? What's he like?'

This was the question Ray had feared and he tried to sound matter-of-fact in his answer.

'Oh, didn't I say? It's not a guy, it's a woman. Her name's Annie Chaplin. Very bright gal in her late thirties. I met her when I was recording some stuff for *Pause for Thought* on Radio Two.'

Ollie couldn't help thinking that there was something just too deliberately off-the-cuff about those words – 'Oh, didn't I say?' He instinctively felt that his dad had deliberately omitted the fact that his new colleague was a woman. His response was to try to sound just as laid-back with his next question: 'And what does Mum think of you proposing to spend the next year working closely with this woman?'

Ray hesitated before he answered. It was one of those moments when a conversation seems to take on a life of its own, when you have to follow where it leads you and let the chips fall where they will.

'Yeah, I've thought about that…'

He paused for a few seconds and tried to avoid looking at Ollie.

'Actually, I haven't told her yet.'

'What – you haven't told her about what you're thinking of doing? Or you haven't told her that you'll be working with a woman?'

There was a second or two of silence in which both men sensed that they were about to get to the nub of this conversation. Ray pushed his chair back a little from the table and put his hands on his knees.

'I haven't told her either of those things. She knows I'm unsettled and she knows I've been working with someone at the BBC. But she's assumed it's just the usual religious broadcasting stuff. So I've left it at that for the moment. It's got a little bit tricky…'

His voice tailed off and he lowered his head and stared at the table. Ollie felt a distinct nervousness come over him, something far stronger and more unpleasant than stage fright. He was aware of his heart beating faster and his throat feeling dry. He unfolded his arms and leaned on the table, afraid to put into words the question that was forming in his mind. For a moment he said nothing. When he did speak, his voice was scarcely more than a whisper: 'Dad, you're worrying me. Is there something you're not telling me?'

For the rest of his life he'd never be able to forget the expression on his dad's face at that moment. It was a look of desolation and loneliness, like the face of a man who's suddenly lost his memory and doesn't know who or where he is any longer. Ray swallowed a couple of times and a tear began to trickle down his face.

'Like I said, it's tricky. Your mum's great and you know how good our marriage has always been. The last thing I want to do is hurt her. But Annie's been really helpful when I've been feeling like I have. I can talk to her about stuff on a different level. She understands what I'm going through...'

He pulled a tissue from his pocket and blew his nose. It occurred to Ollie that he couldn't ever remember seeing his dad cry before.

'And, yes, we have grown close just in these last few weeks. I've wanted to tell your mum about it, but I can't find the right words or the right time, and I don't want to hurt her...'

Whenever Ollie looked back on that moment, he couldn't recall *saying* the words he said next so much as *hearing* himself say them. In his memory it was like a scene from a movie in which the rest of the cast slip out of focus and the buzz of their conversations fades into the background; as if the camera zoomed in on their table and they became the only actors in a drama in which everyone else was just an extra; as if he was reading a sentence that the writer had just inserted into the script without warning, a sentence with strange and unexpected words that were difficult to pronounce.

'Dad, what's so hard about telling Mum that you're working with a woman? It's more than that, isn't it? Have you slept with her?'

Ray looked at the floor for a moment, then nodded several times.

'Yes, I have.'

He wished he could add something that would explain everything in a way that would make some kind of sense to his son. But there was nothing he could say. Ollie persisted with his interrogation and his anger began to surface.

'What does that mean? You've slept with her just once? Or is it more than that? Are you having an affair?'

As he'd driven up to Edinburgh, Ray had half-feared and half-hoped that their conversation would reach this point. His conscious mind warned him to avoid the topic at all costs, but in the depths of his being he knew that he needed to speak truth, to tell someone who might help him find a way through the dangerous emotional road on which he was walking. And somewhere at the back of his mind the idea had begun to form that his son might even empathise in some way. A younger generation, he reasoned, would be much more liberal in these matters, far less prone to condemn, much more likely to understand. His voice was barely audible, but it was as much a cry for help as a confession.

'Yes, it's more than that. I guess we've been sleeping together regularly for a couple of months now.'

He looked across the table. He felt he was throwing himself on his son's mercy hoping for some kind of understanding or empathy.

But Ollie would not – could not – offer sanctuary or shelter. Long-buried memories of childhood injustices at the hands of a strict disciplinarian parent, bitter recollections of teenage confrontations when boy and man had pitted their wills against each other in unequal combat, surging waves of pent-up anger at the harshness of a religion foisted on him and then rejected as legalistic and life-denying – all this swept over Ollie at that moment, driven by a hurricane of explosive indignation at the apparent duplicity of the man sitting opposite him who was negating everything he'd ever claimed to stand for by cheating on his wife. For the first time in his life he swore at his dad and a torrent of expletives poured from his lips.

'You hypocrite!' he shouted. 'You pretend to want to talk to me about "some interesting changes" in your life when all the time you've been messing around with some woman you've met. You lay all this on me when you haven't even had the guts to own up to Mum. You're a total disgrace. I don't ever want to see you or talk to you again. You better sort this out with Mum quick, or I'll tell her what a heel you've been.'

Ray tried to mumble something about how sorry he was and how he just needed some time to sort things out, but his words were lost on Ollie, who pushed his chair back noisily and stood up.

'And you can keep your money,' he said as he threw a £20 note on the table. 'I'll pay for my own breakfast.'

As he spun on his heel and hurried away, he was only dimly conscious of the faces of the drinkers at the bar that had been watching the altercation at the table and were now turned towards him. It wasn't until he pushed his way through the door and back onto the cobbled streets of the Royal Mile that he began to think just how irrevocable the break might be. But that mattered little to him at that moment. He just wanted to put as much distance between them as he could.

By the time Ollie was a couple of hundred yards along the Royal Mile, Ray had gone over to the bar and apologised for the disturbance. 'Just one of those moments that happen in the best of families,' he explained as he settled the bill. He realised after he'd handed over his credit card that it would have been better to have paid with cash and made his escape more speedily. The barman was sensitive enough not to try to make polite conversation, although that only served to make the embarrassed silence around him worse. Even then, he couldn't break the habit of a lifetime as he took a moment to fold the receipt in half and slip it into his wallet. He muttered his thanks and then he headed to the door, trying not to hurry and looking neither to the left nor the right.

# Five

## How Did it Come to This?

Ray walked slowly down from the Royal Mile towards Princes Street where he'd parked his car just off the main thoroughfare. He knew he was in no fit state to drive home straight away, so he sat in the sunshine in the gardens for almost an hour, too numb to think about anything in particular, but vaguely annoyed by the fact that the gardens afforded no real escape from the bustle of the adjoining street. Then on a whim, or perhaps in the hope of getting above the noise of the traffic, he decided to climb the Scott Monument, a structure he'd never liked and whose sombre appearance had scared him on a childhood visit to Edinburgh many years before. He remembered reading in his student days that the local oily sandstone from which the edifice was built had been deliberately chosen because of its propensity to attract dirt. Apparently the architect had wanted it to turn black quickly! The predilection of the neo-gothic movement for all that was dark, sombre and melodramatic was something he'd never been able to appreciate before. Today, however, it seemed to match his dark mood and sense of depression.

He climbed the 287 steps, ignoring the feeling of claustrophobia as the staircase narrowed the higher he went. Once or twice he had to call out from one of the landings to announce his presence since there wasn't even room to squeeze against the wall and allow someone to pass on the way down. The beads of sweat were forming on his forehead and he was beginning to wonder why on earth he'd chosen to pay £4 to visit a monument which was as unpleasant on the inside as it was intimidating on the outside, when he reached the top and was startled by the view that confronted him on all sides. He looked down on the neatly landscaped gardens immediately below and then allowed his eyes to scan the panoramic vista of the city, looking resplendent but, to his eyes on that day, disturbingly ominous in the late morning sunshine.

The castle standing sentinel over the Old Town beneath and looking far more like something that had emerged organically out of the rock through long geological ages rather than a fortress built by human hands across mere centuries; the spire of St Giles' Cathedral struggling to assert itself against the castle rock, as if religion was some kind of afterthought or, at best, just the puny response of our species to the inexorable processes of nature; Holyrood Park, with its resonances of monarchy and hierarchy, all of them ill-fated and short-lived attempts to impose order and meaning on an unpredictable and unfeeling universe; Arthur's Seat, an extinct volcano whose presence so close to the city forced Ray to contemplate the bleak thought that the world we know, far from being the handiwork of a benevolent creator, might be nothing other than the chance by-product of terrible and destructive forces which will one day reassert themselves and release their awesome power to devastating effect all over again; and in the distance the Firth of Forth whose waters shimmered in the sun, but whether that offered the hopeful prospect of escape to far-off welcoming shores or the hideous possibility of extinction in the ultimately hostile environment of a turbulent and merciless sea, he wasn't at all sure. What he did know for certain as he turned to make his way back down, was that life had never seemed to him more bleak and pointless than it did on that morning in Edinburgh.

By the time he'd got to his car, negotiated his way to the outskirts of the city, and set off on the journey south it was already mid-afternoon. The warmth of the sun combined with his exertions in climbing the Scott Monument and the emotional toll of the morning produced in him an overwhelming weariness. He managed to struggle against the tiredness and keep going until he reached the Tebay services where he pulled off the motorway, pushed his seat into a reclining position, and fell into a deep sleep. It was seven o'clock when he drifted back into consciousness and the memory of the day's events gradually seeped back into his mind, an unstoppable rising tide of hopelessness that threatened to submerge his entire being. He remembered that he hadn't eaten since breakfast-time and although he wasn't sure that he was hungry, he told himself that he'd feel better for some food. Having travelled up and down this road countless times, he knew that he would at least have the consolation of eating at one of the very few places on the motorway network that actually sold real food rather than the poor pre-packaged fare that he had to endure so often on his travels.

The cafeteria was fairly quiet at that time of the evening and the girl at the self-service counter was courteous with a pleasant smile but, to his relief, she gave no indication of wanting to make small talk. It didn't take him long to make his choice, and carry his tray to a table far enough away from the handful of other diners, ensuring that the sound of their conversations was no more than a tolerable white noise in the background. There are times in life, he told himself as he took his first mouthful, when a bowl of home-made soup and a couple of slices of wholemeal bread and butter taste better than the finest cuisine in the most expensive restaurant. He ate slowly, savouring every mouthful, gradually reclaiming his place in the world, slowly climbing out of that abyss of lonely subjectivity into which he had descended from time to time for as long as he could remember. He repeated his childhood mantra to himself: 'I'm me: I know I'm me,' mentally reassuring himself that he was Ray Young, he was a *person* negotiating a route through a storm of confusion and sadness rather than someone whose entire identity was being swept away by the misery that was swirling around him. As he continued to eat, the tide of depression began to recede a little, and he tried to put the events, not only of the day, but of the last six months into some sort of order.

He thought back to that day where it had all started and wondered how things had turned out as they had done. If only he'd gone straight home after the recording, not sat around drinking coffee in wet clothes listening to an attractive thirty-something outlining her ideas for a radio series, none of this would have happened. But he'd stayed. It wasn't just that he'd felt some strong sexual chemistry drawing him to her, though with the benefit of hindsight he now knew how real that was. He'd been long enough in pastoral ministry to be aware of his own vulnerability in that area and he'd learned to extricate himself from situations where there was any possibility of succumbing to temptation. And, yes, he had been more than a little flattered by the fact that a girl of that age was showing such interest in a man turning fifty. Those things had obviously been factors in his decision to stay, or more accurately his failure to make the decision to leave.

Even then, it could have been nothing more than a brief encounter, one of those conversations you have with someone where the possibility of working together is raised but no one follows up on it, and the whole thing is soon forgotten. Annie's ideas for a series on why some people come to believe while others completely lose the faith they've held for years were interesting, but no more than that. What had changed everything was the moment she'd accurately identified his own inner struggle, put her finger right on the thing he'd been trying to avoid, articulated what he'd been afraid to admit – that though he was still ticking the boxes and saying the right things, there was no life, no dynamic in his faith. That's why he'd lost control of himself, why his stupid tears had started, why he'd had to get out of the coffee shop, why he'd ended up at her apartment, why he'd allowed himself to be vulnerable, why he'd poured out the whole sorry story of how utterly empty he felt when she'd listened to him without any embarrassment or condemnation. He'd known then that whatever happened next, something significant had changed, life would never be the same again.

Of course, he'd fully intended to tell Jean all about it, talk through his struggles with her, get her take on it. But she was out with a friend when he got home that afternoon, and by the time she got back in the evening, he'd been too exhausted to go through the whole thing again. After that... well, it never seemed to be quite the right moment. And the time drifted on until he was able to persuade himself that maybe it wasn't such a big deal and that there was no point in burdening her with it. He'd just got a bit overemotional and he'd have to work through the doubt and the questions for himself. And when Annie had called a couple of days later, just to ask how he was and whether he thought there was any mileage in her proposal that they work together on the project, he'd agreed to meet with her and explore the ideas she'd shared with him.

At their first meeting they'd briefly drawn up a rough outline of how they might move forward with the project and who they might talk to. But the truth was that they'd talked as much about him and where he was heading as they did about how they might work together. And at the end of the session he was more pleased than he knew he should have been when they'd put another half-dozen dates in their calendars to meet up over the next three months. Between those meetings, to all intents and purposes, his life had at first gone on much as it had done for years. He'd preached on Sunday mornings, he'd presented seminars at a number of regional and denominational conferences, he'd written articles for his blog commenting on the intersection of faith and culture. But the orderly exterior of his life belied the inner turmoil that was increasingly beginning to force its way to the surface.

For a week or two he'd attempted to ignore it. When he could no longer manage to do that he'd tried to suppress it, to distract himself by keeping busy. After a month or so he'd known that something was happening that no amount of willpower alone could hold in check. There was no satisfaction in his work and motivation was becoming an increasing problem. His previously active and fulfilling sex-life with Jean was faltering and more than once he had to mumble an embarrassed apology about feeling unwell or being distracted by an assignment he had to prepare. Instead of sleeping soundly for six or seven hours as he'd typically done, he was finding himself suddenly wide awake at two o'clock in the morning unable to get back to sleep again.

It was on one of those sleepless nights, sitting in his study with a half-finished cup of lukewarm tea and a blank sheet of paper in front of him, that he'd acknowledged that, for the sake of his sanity, he had to face up to what was causing this unprecedented upheaval in his life. Even now, looking across the increasingly deserted motorway café, he could vividly recall the instant when he'd cut through the vague generalisations he'd been making to himself about mid-life crisis, and begun to spell out what was really happening to him. It was a moment of startling lucidity in which two things became clear beyond any doubt. The first was the conclusion he'd long been dreading but from which there was no longer any hiding place: he could no longer with any integrity describe himself as a Christian believer. It just didn't work for him any longer. The doctrines he'd expounded to others were irrelevant and unconvincing to him. Belief in a personal God directing his life was no more than a distant memory. The young man who'd set out in ministry all those years before, passionately determined to change the world and challenge the Church, seemed like a different person.

That alone would have been enough to disturb the balance of his life. But that night in his study he'd admitted to himself for the first time the 'other thing', the pressure that had been building up in him for weeks now: *he couldn't get Annie Chaplin out of his mind.* She was in his thoughts throughout the day, he emailed her or called or on the slightest pretext just so that he could hear her voice, and he looked forward to their meetings with an eagerness that surprised him. Even in moments of intimacy with Jean it was Annie he was thinking about, Annie he was kissing, Annie he was making love to. Of course, he still loved Jean. She was good, faithful, everything a wife should be. They were comfortable together, their lives were bound up together. But this thing with Annie was different. This was an all-consuming passion, something he couldn't ever recall having experienced before, something he knew he'd have to overcome or it would overcome him.

As a man whose thinking had become conditioned to looking for figures of speech and symbols that would give expression to realities that would otherwise remain abstract, his mind began to form a picture of what was happening to him. It was an image of two great tectonic plates pressing against each other, pushing to the surface of his life, and threatening an eruption that might destroy everything. But if physical earthquakes have to take their inevitable course, he'd reasoned, he could and would take action to limit the consequences of this upheaval. There was nothing he could do about his loss of faith other than acknowledge it had happened and move on, but his attraction to Annie Chaplin need not follow an inevitable course. He'd have to end their working relationship and stop meeting her. So by eight o'clock in the morning he'd called her and arranged to meet her in the afternoon. He'd been a little hesitant when she asked if he'd mind coming to her flat as she'd got some workmen in to estimate for some redecoration that she needed doing, but he'd reassured himself that their presence might be no bad thing given the nature of his visit. A couple of hours later he rang her bell just as the decorators were leaving.

He'd planned how the conversation would go on his way from home. He wouldn't beat around the bush, he'd apologise for backing out of the project and explain that he really needed to give more time to working out where his future lay and how he might earn his living. Then he'd leave as quickly as he could. Best not to say anything to Annie about his feelings for her. That way he'd avoid any embarrassment for either of them. Anyway, he'd no reason to believe that she felt the same way about him. It would be brief and painless, he'd be out of there within ten minutes, and the whole thing would be over before it had even got started.

In fact, it didn't work out like that at all. He could smell the aroma from the percolator as soon as the door opened, and she'd had already begun pouring the coffee before he sat down. It was impossible to avoid the initial small talk about the cost of the work to be done and the inevitable inconvenience of having workmen around the place. By the time he'd got to the point of explaining the reason for his visit his earlier confidence was rapidly draining away. He'd tried to go through the speech he'd rehearsed in his mind, but his words felt clumsy and he could see that Annie was finding them unconvincing.

When he'd finished, she'd looked at him with a quizzical half-smile and said simply, 'Ray, what's the real reason? What are you not saying?'

Immediately he'd recalled the impact of her words that first afternoon in the coffee shop and he knew that she had broken through his guard once again. She'd cut off his escape route and there was no way he could think of to skirt round the issue. He had no option but to tell the truth.

'Annie, my faith has fallen apart and I've no real idea what I'm going to do about that. Being with you and doing the stuff we've been doing has made that clearer than ever to me. But that's not my biggest problem. Being with you is just too difficult…'

She'd looked at him with an intensity that had made him nervous. He'd no idea how she'd respond to what he was about to say and, truth to tell, he hadn't been sure how he wanted her to react, but he knew that he'd gone too far down the path to turn back.

'Annie, I really like you. In fact, I like you too much. I think about you too much. I like you in a way that's inappropriate for a married man. I can't trust myself to meet up with you. I shouldn't really be here now and I ought to leave.'

He'd wanted to say something else that would close the conversation but before he could think of it, she'd leaned forward and put her hand on his. Very quietly she said, 'Ray, do you mean you're in love with me?'

It was a moment he'd hoped to avoid at all costs. At least, that's what he thought he'd hoped. Now he wasn't sure what he'd been hoping for. But he'd nowhere to hide any longer. He'd made his last move and now it was checkmate. He'd answered her question with one word: 'Yes'. Annie had just smiled and clasped his hand tighter.

'I wanted you to say that,' she whispered. 'In fact, I've wanted you to say it for weeks now.'

Sitting in the Tebay services now, looking out as dusk was falling on an August evening, Ray reflected on the import of those two simple sentences spoken just a few months before, and how they had changed everything for ever. A line had been crossed, a line he'd never thought he would step over. It was Annie who had made the first move when she leaned closer and hugged him. He'd responded with a warm embrace that passed very quickly to a fiercely passionate kiss. Before either of them had fully realised what was happening they'd moved from the lounge to Annie's bedroom. It was to be just the first time of many that they would make love there over the coming weeks. They'd continued to work together on Annie's project and had even made some progress in charting out the format for half a dozen programmes and lining up a number of people to interview. But what mattered most to them was just to be together. The desire that was driving their relationship had become all-consuming. It was a tsunami that swept everything before it – the moral code by which he'd lived, the strictures of conscience that previously would have troubled him so deeply, his loyalty to Jean that had mattered so much to him – all crumbled under the onslaught of an unstoppable passion.

Of course, there was the persistent niggle at the back of his mind telling him that things couldn't go on like this, that sooner or later there would be conversations to be had and decisions to be made. That was why he'd made the trip to Edinburgh to talk to Ollie, even though he'd had little idea of how that particular conversation would go or how it would end. He'd harboured some kind of wild hope that, moving in the kind of circles he did, Ollie might understand or at least point him to a way out of his dilemma. But the truth was out now and his son's reaction to his revelation left him in no doubt that he could no longer put off the thing he most dreaded in all the world. He'd have to talk to Jean and tell her what was really going on.

As he left the motorway café and walked to his car he could hear the cawing of the rooks and just make out the dark shadow of their flight as they went to roost for the night. It was a sight and sound that never failed to disturb him. He reminded himself that he didn't believe in omens and portents, but it made little difference. His mood that had lightened a little as he'd eaten, darkened again very quickly. As he turned back onto the motorway, he knew he had a long dark road ahead of him before he'd be home again.

# Six

## A Day in Auld Reekie

When he stormed out of Prince Charlie's Tipple, Ollie's first thought had been to get drunk. Totally blathered. Just blot out the rest of the day and lose himself in a booze-induced haze of forgetfulness. His mind was a turmoil of confused and conflicting emotions: anger with his father for his selfishness, sympathy for his mother, whose desolation when she found out he could only imagine, alarm at the intensity of the fury that had taken hold of him in the pub. And most difficult of all for him to come to terms with, the overwhelming disappointment he felt – felt it like the taste of something rancid in his mouth – at his father's betrayal of the beliefs and principles he'd professed to hold all his life. OK, he might have rebelled against his upbringing and rejected that kind of faith himself. But it was one thing to think that those who claimed allegiance to a faith and its moral compass were old-fashioned or misguided; it was quite another to face the possibility that all along they'd been engaging in an elaborate and pious pretence. You could still respect and trust a man who was sincerely and devoutly mistaken; you could only despise a man who turned out to be a hypocrite.

And somehow or other, for Ollie, that threatened to erode any hope that life just might make sense, that there might be some genuine goodness at the very heart of things. A couple of hours ago his mood had matched a day that was bright and full of promise. Now the warmth of the sun served only to make him aware of how cold he felt inside. It reminded him of a fever he'd had as a child when he'd thrown off the bedclothes, unable to understand how his skin could feel so unbearably hot while he was shivering on the inside.

He needed a drink and he needed it quick. So he turned right and headed in the direction of the castle knowing from experience that there would be no shortage of suitable watering holes along the route where he could sit in a dark corner and drown his sorrows. By now the Royal Mile was teeming with people filling the city for the Festival, and progress, he realised, was going to be slower than his thirst and his mood demanded. He vented his irritation on a couple of tourists walking in the opposite direction who managed to bump into him, meeting their profuse apology with a curt, 'Aw, shut up!' His frustration threatened to boil over when he drew level with a popular coffee shop and had to step to the side to avoid a group of about twenty people gathered round a young woman with a white T-shirt who was checking their names off on her clipboard. 'Just another boring tour guide,' he muttered to himself. Despite his annoyance, he noted that there was sure to be an abundance of good comic material to be drawn from observing such a pointless middle-class and middle-aged activity. He'd have to make sure he went on one of those tours before he left Edinburgh.

He was about to hurry on, when it registered that there was something familiar about the tour guide. He turned and took a closer look. To his surprise and delight it was the girl with the copper-coloured hair. It was one of those 'do I, don't I?' moments when he hesitated, wondering whether he should stop or just keep going. After all, he wasn't in the best of spirits and she obviously wasn't in a situation where she was likely to succumb to his ready supply of well-rehearsed chat-up lines. But when she called out, 'Is there anybody else joining us? Last chance to join the most informative and entertaining walking tour on the Royal Mile,' his mind was made up instantly. Maybe a miserable day was about to take a turn for the better. And looking at a pretty girl had the potential to be a far more effective antidepressant than even a double whisky or three. He raised his hand and called back from the edge of the group, 'You can add me to your list.'

The tour guide glanced up from her clip board and was about to ask for the name of the latest recruit to her walking party, when she recognised Ollie. Her face broke into a smile and she gave a mock bow in his direction.

'No need to ask your name,' she said with a laugh.

Then, with an exaggerated theatrical wave of her hand, she announced to the rest of her company, 'Ladies and gentlemen, we are privileged indeed to be joined by one of the luminaries of this year's Fringe, an up-and-coming star of the comedy scene. Give it up, if you will, for Mr Ollie Oldham.'

Ollie responded to the applause that followed her announcement with a bow, though he hadn't the slightest doubt that the predominantly middle-aged crowd was responding to the charms of the young woman about to lead them on their sight-seeing expedition rather than registering their recognition of a Manchester lad just beginning to break through on the comedy circuit. He thought to himself that this was probably the first time in his life that he didn't have the slightest feeling of resentment that the ovation was directed towards someone other than himself.

His assessment of the situation proved to be accurate, for as soon as the copper-haired girl spoke again the attention of his fellow tourists was turned immediately back on her.

'Let me introduce myself. I'm Ellen Kilpatrick and it's my privilege to be your tour guide here on the Royal Mile. I'm a poor student coming up to my final year of an MA in philosophy and politics at Edinburgh university. But in the summer months this is what I do to save myself from poverty and starvation.'

She delivered the last sentence with a twinkle in her eye and a tremor in her voice which elicited a collective 'Aah' from her audience.

'Well, thank you for your sympathy,' she added, wiping an imaginary tear from her eye. 'But remember, talk's cheap. You can demonstrate your compassion for this poor undergraduate by giving generously at the end of the tour. Now let's get started.'

Ollie could detect from her accent that she'd been born and raised somewhere in the north of Scotland rather than being a native of Edinburgh. Her speech had an easy clarity and a lilting cadence to it that complemented her striking appearance. It penetrated the noise of the street without any need to shout. He'd heard his dad do his exaggerated impersonation of the Highlander's 'teuchter' accent with its dialect features which seemed to provide ready amusement for lowland Scots. But there was nothing comic about the voice he was hearing now. The softened consonants and distinctive vowel sounds served only to captivate his attention and make her all the more attractive. Everything about her gave the impression of a young woman who probably managed to be both academically successful and generally popular with her peers, especially those of the opposite sex.

His interest had certainly been awakened the day before in the pub. Now that he could see and hear her in the light of a summer's day, he was definitely intrigued. A guided tour of the Royal Mile had never previously figured in his bucket list. Now he felt that ninety minutes of architectural observations and historical anecdotes was a small price to pay just to stand within a few feet of this woman who'd captured his attention. She might even manage to keep him from thinking about the conversation he'd just had with his dad.

The next hour and a half passed quickly. Ellen Kilpatrick had mastered her material and had a facility to ad lib that Ollie couldn't help but admire. Beginning with an amusing explanation to a couple of confused Londoners that 'reek' was a good old Scottish word for smoke, and that Edinburgh's nickname of 'Auld Reekie' was a reference to the days when coal fires would leave a heavy dark pall hanging over the city, she led her followers up the Royal Mile towards the castle. They set off from the Mercat Cross, a place historically associated with public proclamations and unpleasant punishments, and Ollie's disenchantment with organised religion wasn't helped by the tale of the devout but unfortunate Sir James Tarbet whose penalty in 1565 for daring to conduct Mass had been to be tied to a cross and pelted by eggs. He managed to offend a group from America's Bible Belt with his comment that since most of the religious people he knew were hypocrites, that was better treatment than many of them deserved.

Things got even worse when they reached the site of the ancient Tolbooth Prison and Ellen invited them to observe the time-honoured custom of spitting on the heart set into the cobblestones where the entrance to the jail had once stood. The party of devout American tourists, who had been proudly proclaiming their Scottish heritage alongside their allegiance to the King James Bible until that point, decided that they'd seen enough of their ancestors' strange customs and set off in search of lunch and more civilised company.

All this delighted Ollie who was even managing to push the unpleasant events of the morning to the back of his mind. There was more to this guided tour scam, he thought to himself, than just a dreary procession past some ancient monuments. Ellen had a rich fund of colourful stories which made it much more entertaining than the dull, dry history trips he remembered from school days. If the looming presence of St Giles' Cathedral and the references to the Scottish Reformation and the fiery preaching of John Knox threatened to cast the dark shadow of religion over his mood again, her mischievous retelling of the story of Deacon Brodie, an Edinburgh worthy in the eighteenth century, soon dispelled the gloom. The tale of this seemingly respectable pillar of society who lived a double life appealed to Ollie's heightened sense of the frailties and follies of humanity.

A family man and town councillor by day, under cover of night Brodie revealed his true character. His frequent visits to Edinburgh's notorious fleshpots, indulging his appetite for gambling, drinking and womanising, would have been enough to stretch the finances of any man to the limits. But Brodie's expenses also included maintaining three families – his legal wife and children as well as two mistresses and their illegitimate offspring – all living within the radius of a mile without knowing anything of each other's existence! Since he knew of no lawful way of funding that kind of extravagant lifestyle, Brodie resorted to burgling the homes of his wealthy acquaintances. In the end, after a particularly daring raid on His Majesty's Excise Office, he was betrayed by one of the members of his gang who informed on him on the promise of a free pardon. He was brought to trial and sentenced to death by hanging. But Brodie wasn't a man to bow out quietly. His arrogance undiminished, and dressed in his Sunday best, he arrived at the Tolbooth where a crowd of 40,000 was waiting to witness the spectacle. By the bloodthirsty standards of the time, they were regally entertained as the gallows failed to function properly and the drop had to be reset three times before justice was administered to the condemned man.

Ellen brought the story to a conclusion with the wry comment that times had changed, of course, and none of our present town councillors would ever be guilty of such illegal or immoral practices. The reaction of her audience to that statement made it abundantly clear that they definitely didn't share her confidence in the moral rectitude of today's public figures, and their cynicism was enough to jolt Ollie out of his good humour of the last half hour and back into the dark mood that the earlier revelations of the morning had produced in him. His dad was just another one in a long line of shabby hypocrites, he thought to himself.

As they continued up the Royal Mile, Ellen pointed out the various buildings and landmarks and recited an impressive litany of Scottish writers and men of letters – Burns, Scott, Stevenson, Boswell, Hume – but the imposing architecture and the splendour of the nation's literary past was completely lost on Ollie as the depression of the morning threatened to engulf him again. It was only his hope that there might be a chance to get to know his guide better that kept him from slipping away to the nearest pub.

Eventually they reached the Castle Esplanade where the tour concluded to a round of spontaneous applause and a bagful of generous contributions from Ellen's grateful audience. A dozen or so of them lined up to shake her hand and Ollie deliberately waited at the end of the line, willing the last few stragglers to get on their way and leave him alone with the young woman who was the centre of their and his attention. At last she was on her own and he took his opportunity.

'That was great,' he said. 'I'm not especially into the tourist sight-seeing thing, but you're really good at working an audience. I can see I'll need to ask you for a few lessons.'

She looked at him with the kind of knowing smile that left him in no doubt she wasn't about to be easily swayed by his compliments.

'Aye, that'll be right,' she replied. 'You're a professional. I'm just doing this to make enough cash to pay the bills and see me through my studies. And, if you don't mind me mentioning it again, talk's cheap. You haven't coughed up any money yet and I've got to eat. This tour guide stuff is hungry work.'

Ollie laughed at her blunt rebuttal.

'*Touché*,' he responded as he pulled out his wallet and dropped in a £5 note with a theatrical flourish.

'And I can do better than that,' he went on. 'Let me treat you to lunch. I know a nice little place not far from here.'

For a moment she looked at him suspiciously without saying a word and he thought she was about to refuse his offer. But then she seemed to be satisfied that his intentions were honourable enough.

'OK,' she laughed. 'If you're paying, I'm coming.'

She slung her leather bag containing her morning's takings over her shoulder and slipped her arm into his.

'So where are we heading, kind sir?'

He led the way to a little café just off the Royal Mile where they shared a lunch of soup and smoked mackerel bagels. Ellen explained that she'd started her day with just a quick cup of coffee, so conversation would have to wait until she'd eaten. Ollie, who couldn't quite believe that a day that had started out so badly had taken such a turn for the better, was quite prepared to be patient and bide his time. He contented himself with a few pleasantries until their plates were cleared. But the arrival of coffee gave him the opportunity to get beyond small talk and come straight to the point.

'I noticed you at my lunchtime show yesterday,' he began.

'It's never easy for me to keep a low profile with hair the colour of mine,' she admitted. 'I do tend to stand out in a crowd.'

'It wasn't just that. I mean, your hair *is* very attractive. But I wanted to say hello and you left before the end.'

'Oh, I get it. You thought a red-head would make an easy target for your patter.'

'Naah, I wanted to say hello. Talk to you, maybe buy you a drink, get to know you. I thought you were really nice.'

Ellen gave him what he imagined his mum would have described as an 'old-fashioned look' that served instantly to deflate his normal self-confidence. This was going very differently to his usual encounters with the opposite sex. As chat-up lines went, these were certainly not the sharpest he'd ever used, and it came as something of a shock to him to realise that he was actually trying to be honest rather than smart. Suddenly he felt clumsy and even a little shy. He desperately wanted to say something witty and claw back the initiative in the conversation, but he couldn't think of anything. For the first time he could remember in a very long time he was tongue-tied. For a moment they sat looking at each other until Ellen broke into a fit of laughter.

'You're *funny*,' she said when she stopped laughing. 'You crack me up.'

'Well, it's what I do for a living. I make people laugh.'

'I don't mean *that* kind of funny – though you are. I mean you're *funny* when you don't mean to be. Like a little kid who's been caught out. Like you're trying to sound more confident than you really are…'

Once again he found himself on the defensive. And once again he realised he was revealing the truth about himself.

'Maybe you're on to something there. There's got to be some kind of insecurity that makes guys like me travel round the country, trying to make people that they don't know and probably won't ever meet again laugh, trying to get complete strangers to like us.'

'Is chatting up penniless tour guides and buying them lunch the same kind of thing?' Ellen asked. 'You just want somebody to like you?'

For a man who was trying to make a career out of being clever and funny with the English language, Ollie knew he was losing control of this exchange of words. If it had been a chess game the young woman sitting across the table would have been calling 'check'. He knew he was cornered. So he decided to go for broke.

'Maybe. Or maybe it's a little more specific. Maybe I want *you* to like me.'

He meant the words to sound off-the-cuff and light-hearted, but as soon as he'd said them he knew he'd made himself even more vulnerable. Would she think he was some kind of needy celebrity wanna-be who looked for affirmation wherever he could get it? Or would she just find him weird and head straight for the door? To his great relief, she didn't move other than to settle herself a little more comfortably in her chair.

'I've got half an hour before I've got to get ready for an afternoon tour. So you can buy me another coffee and tell me about yourself, and I'll make up my mind whether I like you or not.'

Ollie had no doubts that this was a price worth paying for the chance to spend a little longer in Ellen's company. So when the waitress had brought the coffee he launched into his story. She let him talk without interrupting, other than to ask a few questions and make the appropriate responses. He told her more, and in greater detail, than he'd really meant to – his shyness as a kid, his discovery that being the class joker was the way to overcome it, his churchy upbringing, his teenage rebellion, dropping out of university, getting into stand-up – though he stopped short at relating the morning's encounter with his father at Prince Charlie's Tipple. He'd been talking pretty well non-stop for forty minutes when he glanced at his watch.

'Sorry,' he said. 'I didn't mean to go on as long. Now you know all about me.'

'I'm sure it's not *all*,' she answered with a heavy emphasis on the last word. 'But it'll do to be going on with. And I really need to be going. Thanks for lunch. I've really enjoyed it.'

As she took hold of her bag and got ready to leave, the afternoon sun shone through the window highlighting the intense copper tones of Ellen's hair and contrasting it with her fair complexion. A half-forgotten childhood memory suddenly flooded back into his mind. As a six-year-old boy, he'd seen a picture in a magazine of a young woman, dressed in a flowing white nightgown, combing her vivid red hair in front of a mirror. To the amusement of his parents, the realistic photographic technique of the artist had fascinated him to such an extent that they found out it was by the American portrait painter, William McGregor Paxton, and bought a reproduction. It hung on a wall at home until his early teenage years when their teasing comments about 'Ollie's girlfriend' embarrassed him to the point where he'd demanded they take it down. It sat in the garage for a couple of years until it was eventually sent to the local Oxfam shop.

He must have been staring at her in that unselfconscious way that children often do but that adults regard as an indication of oddness, because she said a little nervously, 'Why are you staring at me like that?

'I'm sorry,' he said, jolting himself back into the moment. 'I didn't mean to stare. It's just you reminded me of a painting I used to like when I was a kid. I'd forgotten all about it until now. I'll tell you about it if you agree to meet me again.'

Ellen pulled a face that was meant to give an impression of incredulity.

'I remind you of a painting, eh? What's this guy gonna say next?'

Ollie thought he'd blown it, but she pulled a pen and a scrap of paper out of her bag.

'I'd like to meet *you* again,' she said as she quickly scribbled her mobile number down. 'But I really am running late. Give me a call tomorrow sometime and we'll sort something out.'

She patted him on the arm as she pushed open the door. Ollie watched her through the window of the café as she hurried along the street. Then he sat for a moment or two before he got up to leave. It was turning out to be a day of very different encounters and contrasting emotions. He walked slowly out of the café and into the sunshine. He'd need to clear his head before tonight's gig.

# Seven

# The Long Dark Road

It was getting on for eleven o'clock when Ray arrived home. He'd been playing over in his mind for the last 100 miles the conversation he'd need to have with Jean and he knew that there was no way of making it painless for either of them. Better to say nothing tonight. She'd only have got back from Bournemouth an hour or so ago, so she'd be too tired anyway. Try and sound natural and chatty, ask her about her visit to her sister, give her a sanitised version of his meeting with Ollie, and get to bed. That way she'd at least have a decent night's sleep before he dropped the bombshell. And if he couldn't sleep himself, he could easily make the excuse of needing to sit up and finish some work. His heart was beating against his chest as he got out of the car and walked to the front door. He took some deep breaths in an attempt to calm himself and turned his key in the lock.

'Jean, I'm back,' he called out, trying to sound as normal as possible.

The sound of his voice was immediately countered by the piercing whistle of the burglar alarm. He hit the keypad on the wall and stopped the noise. Obviously Jean wasn't at home. He'd assumed that she was there because the lights were on. But, of course, they always set timers when they were away for a couple of days to discourage would-be intruders. He felt an immediate sense of relief that he didn't have to face her tonight. And her absence was no reason to worry. Probably she'd decided to stay an extra day with her sister. They saw each other only once or twice a year, so visits often got extended by a day or two. Just to make sure, he checked the answer-phone, but there were no messages. He was about to pick up the phone and call when he realised the time and decided they'd have gone to bed since she'd be intending to set off first thing in the morning. Well, it was probably for the best. He'd be less tired and less emotional after a night's rest. And, with traffic and a couple of stops on the road, Jean wouldn't be home until mid-afternoon. She'd want to have a nap then. They could talk after that.

He kicked off his shoes and wandered through to the kitchen to make a cup of tea before he went to bed. As he waited for the kettle to boil he forced himself to acknowledge the truth that he'd been avoiding – he didn't know where he wanted their conversation to go. The rational part of him knew what he ought to do. He should apologise to Jean, tell her that he loved her, admit that he'd been a fool, ask her forgiveness and promise to end the affair. But the rational part of him wasn't in control any longer. He was in the grip of a passion which dominated his every waking moment. The pang of guilt he felt each time he left Annie inevitably gave way over the next day or so to a persistent and irresistible longing to see her again. He'd be in the middle of a presentation to a group of church leaders, saying all the right things and to all intents and purposes in charge of the situation. All the while, however, his mind would be filled with fantasies and images that would have shocked his audience had they been able to read his true thoughts.

He'd just made the tea and was about to reach into the fridge for the milk when the doorbell rang. That must be Jean. She's come home tonight after all, he thought, though he couldn't figure out why she was ringing the bell. She always had a house key attached to her car keys. Then he remembered that if someone left their key on the inside of the lock you couldn't get your key in from the outside. He was always doing it and she was always getting annoyed with him for his absent-mindedness. Of course, he must have done it again. At least it would give the impression that everything was normal. Same old Ray, he could hear her saying. And he'd make his usual excuse that his head was so full of important things that he could be forgiven for making such a simple mistake.

But when he reached the front door his key wasn't in the lock. It took him a few seconds to find it at the bottom of the stairs where he must have dropped it when he came in. Why didn't she let herself in? He called out to her as he unlocked the door, grateful for the chance to sound jovial and natural.

'I'll bet you've been shopping with that sister of yours and your hands are full of stuff you've been buying with my hard-earned cash.'

His attempt to give the impression of domestic good humour was cut short by the sight that greeted him when he opened the door. Two police officers, a sergeant and a young constable, stood in front of him. His heart missed a beat. Their presence at this late hour was ominous.

'Mr Ray Young?' the younger policeman asked.

'Yes, I am.'

He was finding it difficult to breathe, and forming those three simple words seemed an almost impossible task.

'May we come in, please?'

He beckoned them into the hallway, not quite sure what to do or say next.

'It would be best if we could sit down, Mr Young.'

They followed him into the kitchen where the three of them sat around the table.

'I'm afraid we have some very bad news for you, Mr Young.'

Ray felt alone and afraid at that moment. When he spoke his voice sounded to him as if it was coming from someone else he barely knew and from some other place a long way off.

'It's my wife, isn't it?' he said. 'Something's happened to her.'

He could see that the constable was very nervous. He guessed it was the first time he'd had to do anything like this.

'Yes, it has, I'm afraid.'

The sergeant gestured to his colleague that he would take over from there.

'Mr Young, I'm sorry to have to inform you that there's been an accident just before junction 19 on the north-bound carriageway of the M6 earlier this evening and your wife was killed. She was still alive when the paramedics got there and they air-lifted her to North Staffordshire

Hospital, but they were unable to save her life. She was dead on arrival at hospital.'

Ray tried one last desperate throw of the dice.

'Are you absolutely sure it's my wife? Could there be some mistake?'

The sergeant's response was sympathetic but his unambiguous assertion left no room for hope.

'We will need you to make a formal identification. But we're certain that the victim is your wife. I am so sorry that this has happened. It must be a great shock to you.'

Ray could never recollect the rest of that conversation in any detail. He had no idea how long it had lasted and he had no memory of the police officers leaving the house. Whenever he looked back on it, it seemed to him that he'd been a stunned observer rather than a concerned participant. He knew he must have asked how the accident had happened because he remembered they'd said that she'd driven into the back of a lorry that had pulled out of the Knutsford Services. And they must have asked him if he wanted them to inform anyone else because he could recall hearing a voice that he dimly recognised as his own adamantly refusing their help and insisting that he would let other people know. The rest of that night was a blur, a bewildering confusion of recriminations and regrets that turned the long dark hours into a barren landscape of empty sadness over which the chill wind of a savage guilt began to blow relentlessly.

It was only when the first light of dawn began to filter through the window that he roused himself from a night of fitful sleep punctuated by disturbing dreams. At first he couldn't think where he was until he realised he was still in the kitchen. The two chairs on which the police officers had been sat were still askew just as his unexpected guests had left them. He must have fallen asleep with his head on the table. As soon as he woke, the reality of his situation hit him like a bucket of icy cold water. *Jean was dead*, lying in a hospital mortuary, and he'd have to go and identify her. He was utterly alone with his conscience and the unbearable thought that he'd never be able to put things right with his wife.

In his days as a local pastor he'd helped people to understand and negotiate their way through the normal initial impact of grief – denial, anger, the inevitable 'if only' questions, the desperate sense of loss. But for him at that moment there was none of that. Just an overwhelming, all-encompassing sense of raw guilt. He'd been cheating on the woman to whom he'd been married for half a lifetime. He hadn't had the courage to tell her the truth about what was going on. He didn't know – not even now – if he would have ended the relationship with Annie after his conversation with Jean. His intended confession might well have turned out to be a callous goodbye rather than an act of contrition. That would have hurt Jean even more than the affair itself. If the accident hadn't killed her, the shock and grief caused by his selfishness would have destroyed her life. His mind was locked in an interminable loop of shame and self-loathing.

It was gone seven o'clock before he could summon the energy to move from the table. The first thing he had to do was to call the family – Jean's sister, Christine, in Bournemouth, his own brother and sister, Tommy and Mary, up in Glasgow. That would be difficult enough. But then there was Ollie. How on earth would he tell his son? Any conversation would have been hard going after their confrontation yesterday. But this didn't bear thinking about. He forced himself to shower and change his clothes. It gave him time to compose himself a little and screw up the courage to pick up the phone. He managed to get through the first two calls to family. They, of course, knew nothing of his relationship with Annie and their reactions were simply of shock and sympathy for Ray. The worst thing, as he listened to their condolences and offers of support, was the duplicity of his own words that left the bitter aftertaste of hypocrisy in his mouth.

He delayed calling Ollie as long as he could, rehearsing in his mind how he could break the news. He even tried writing down what he needed to say and repeating it over to himself, but he couldn't put his words in any sensible order. There was nothing else for it. It had to be done. Ollie needed to know. He picked up the phone and heard it ring out five or six times. He knew Ollie would still be in bed. At the best of times he wouldn't be in a good humour at this hour of the morning. After yesterday's clash, Ray expected the worst. When Ollie eventually answered, he knew that his fears were well-founded.

'Hello, this is Ollie Oldham. Whoever it is, you'd better have a good reason for calling me at this unearthly hour.'

'Son, it's your dad here,' Ray said quietly.

'What do you want?' Ollie demanded. 'I don't want to talk to you until you've sorted things out with Mum.'

'You've got tolisten to me,' Ray pleaded. 'We need to talk. I've got some very bad news.'

'Can't be worse than what you told me yesterday. What've you done now? Got involved with some other cheap tart you've met on one of your preaching gigs?'

Ray began to cry for the first time since the visit of the police officers.

'Don't, please,' he sobbed. 'This is hard enough for me. It's very bad news. Your mum was killed last night driving home from visiting your Aunt Christine.'

There were a few seconds of silence that seemed like an eternity. He tried to fill the gap in the conversation by saying something to bridge the chasm between them.

'I know I've let you down, but we're going to need each other now. We need to stick together.'

Ollie began swearing hysterically down the phone. He couldn't make out every word, but the last couple of sentences were clear enough.

'If this is some kind of stupid trick to get my sympathy, I'll never speak to you again.'

'Ollie, please calm down. I need you to come home. There was a collision with a lorry, but I don't know any other details of the accident. I've got to go and identify Mum's body this morning. There'll have to be a post-mortem. Then we need to arrange the funeral…'

He could hear Ollie crying on the other end of the phone. His words came in short bursts through his tears.

'OK, I'll be home today. We'll deal with this together… but only out of respect for Mum… After that we're through… I'll never forgive you for what you've done. I need to clear up some things here… then I'll be on my way.'

There was a click as Ollie ended the call abruptly.

Ray stood for a few minutes, struggling to get his thoughts into some kind of order. There were things to be done. Go to the hospital and identify Jean's body. Then there would be a post-mortem and, he assumed, an inquest. When would that all happen? What would he need to do? When would her body be released? When could they arrange the funeral? Jean had always been the one who'd sorted out the details of their life together. She'd organised his calendar and made sure he got to the right place on the right day. He wasn't even sure where she'd filed their personal documents. She'd told him countless times that he should take an interest 'in case I'm not around some day'. But he'd always laughed it off. Told her that would be the least of his worries when she'd gone. Now he knew those words were truer than he'd realised when he said them. He didn't know which way to turn. He remembered all the times he'd officiated at funerals and realised that he'd given very little thought to the fact that his role had been only one piece in the jigsaw that people had to put in place at a time when they were too blinded by tears to be able to see the path they were supposed to follow.

He got through the day with the help of Tim Johnson, an Anglican vicar who'd been his most trusted friend for the last twenty years. He'd talked to him about his struggles with faith over the last couple of years and Tim had listened patiently without resorting to the glib responses and easy answers that others might have offered. As soon as Ray called him to let him know what had happened he dropped everything and came round.

'I'm so sorry, mate,' he said as he grabbed him in what they always described jokingly as a holy hug. 'You've been a great husband and you'll miss Jean terribly. I'll do whatever I can to support you through this time. I've cancelled everything for the rest of the week. So I'll help you get done whatever you need to do.'

'Thanks, Tim,' Ray responded, holding on to him tightly. 'And you know I'll want you to conduct the funeral.'

Ray was aware of something breaking deep within him as he said those words. Tim guided him to a chair where he slumped with his head in his hands, great racking sobs convulsing his body. When he did manage to speak, the whole sorry story of his affair with Annie tumbled out. It was a good ten minutes before the deluge of words and tears subsided. He felt drained of every ounce of energy. When Tim responded his words carried no condemnation.

'Well, thanks for trusting me with that. We can talk about it later. For now, you need some rest before you can do anything else. I'll get in touch with the hospital and arrange a time to do what you have to do. I'll drive you there. Let me help you up to bed.'

That was the last thing Ray could remember before Tim roused him a couple of hours later with a cup of tea and told him that he'd fixed a time for them to identify Jean's body that afternoon.

'Oh, and I took the liberty of phoning Ollie just to check on his progress. It took him a bit of time to cancel his shows for the rest of the Festival, but he reckons he should get away from Edinburgh in an hour or so. He's got a key so if we're not back by the time he gets home he can let himself in.'

Ray nodded his thanks and took the tea. He was grateful to have someone to help him through an afternoon he was dreading.

In the event, the visit to the hospital morgue was less traumatic than he'd anticipated. The staff were courteous and sensitive and Tim stayed close to him, making sure he was OK. There was no surge of emotion when he came to view the body, just a sense of numb resignation and cold regret. For a few minutes he stood looking at his wife's body. It was some comfort to him that Jean's face had not been disfigured in any way. That would make it a little bit easier for Ollie, he thought. He had an almost overwhelming urge to kneel down and beg her forgiveness for the mess he'd made of things. But his deep-rooted Scottish reserve was enough to stop that impulse in its tracks. All he did was to bend over and kiss his wife on the forehead. Then he turned around, quickly left the room, and headed along the corridor and back to the hospital car park.

All the way back to Manchester in the car there was a Randy Newman song playing over and over again in his head. He and Jean were both fans of Newman's whimsical turn of phrase and quirky take on things. This one, however, had been a constant source of disagreement between them over the years. The lyrics focused on the fact that whereas when you're young you've got all the time in the world to heal and get on with life, when you're older there just isn't enough time to get over tragedy and loss. Jean loved it and would cry when she heard it, but he'd

always been disparaging about it. Sentimental tosh, he
called it. That, he now realised, had been just a cover-up
for his fear of loss.

Now it seemed to him that they were the most
ruthlessly honest lyrics ever written about life and loss.

# Eight

## Partings

The days immediately following Jean's death passed in a haze of broken sleep, strange dreams, and half-remembered conversations. One day merged into another for Ray without any clear sense of passing time. It was like being in the eye of a hurricane where everything was still and oddly calm, but where his awareness of the powerful storm raging all around him left him feeling ill at ease and fearful of what might happen at any moment. Tim took over the running of things – making phone calls, dealing with messages from friends and colleagues as word of what had happened leaked out, and consulting him only briefly on the arrangements that had to be made.

Ollie returned to the family home for just a few hours on the first evening after arriving from Edinburgh to pick up some clothes that he thought he'd need for the funeral. His red eyes and ashen face revealed how the loss of his mother had impacted him. Ray tried to speak to him and tell him how sorry he was, how he regretted his actions, how he wished he could live the past six months over again. He listened passively to his dad, avoiding eye contact and saying nothing other than that he'd decided to stay with an old school friend who had a flat in Salford.

Tim, who'd known father and son for a long time and was well aware of the tension that often characterised their relationship, walked to the front door with him.

'I know this is really hard for you both, and the next few days aren't going to be easy,' he said quietly. 'If you don't feel you can talk to your dad at the moment, feel free to call me.'

Ollie nodded in acknowledgement of Tim's offer and walked quickly to his car. He couldn't bear to spend any longer than necessary with his dad in the house where he'd been raised. And he'd no intention of ever returning.

The post-mortem examination revealed that Jean's injuries were consistent with the typical physical trauma of that kind of impact collision and the coroner was able to release her body after a couple of days. It came as a relief to Ray that there wouldn't be a lengthy delay and the arrangements for the funeral could go ahead for the middle of the following week. It also roused him sufficiently from the lethargy that had engulfed him for him to deal with the things that Tim couldn't do for him. There were two jobs that needed to be done right away. First, he called Annie and told her of Jean's death. She was working in Wales recording a couple of programmes due to be broadcast later in the year and hadn't heard the news. He was taken aback at the effect it had on her. Her voice was breaking as she tried to speak. He hadn't prepared himself for that kind of reaction and it quickly disarmed the emotional guard he'd tried to put up.

'We can't talk now,' he said fighting back the tears. 'But we need to meet as soon as you get back.'

'I can finish here in the next couple of hours and come straight home tonight,' she responded.

They agreed to meet at her flat the next morning. She spoke so quietly that Ray wasn't sure if he'd heard her correctly, but he thought he could make out the words 'I'll always love you' as he put the phone down.

He slept for an hour after speaking to Annie and then spent the rest of the day into the early hours of the following morning on the second task he was determined to complete – sending out emails cancelling all the speaking commitments in his calendar. With each one he included a very brief personal note apologising for withdrawing from the engagement. But the bulk of his communication was the letter he attached explaining his decision to end a ministry that had been his life for so many years. It took him a long time to put it together. He tried to be as honest as he could without saying more than he had to and he finished the final sentence with a mixture of regret and relief. A ministry he had once loved and found so fulfilling was at an end, but at last he could be released from the increasingly exhausting burden of living a lie. He read the letter over one final time:

Dear Friends,

I write to tell you that I have decided to withdraw with immediate effect from public ministry as a speaker and teacher.

You may by this time have heard of the tragic and untimely death of my wife, Jean, in a road accident recently. This in itself would have necessitated a period of retreat as I try to readjust to life and come to terms with such an overwhelming personal loss. I am deeply grateful to everyone who has already sent messages of sympathy and assured me of their prayers.

However, I confess that for some considerable time now – even before Jean's death – I have been in a place mentally, emotionally, and spiritually where I can no longer give honest and full assent to matters of belief and doctrine which many would consider central to the Christian faith. In addition, there are areas of my personal life that could be questioned if subjected to close scrutiny and to which I need to give serious attention. Consequently, I am painfully aware that I cannot simply continue in my present role with any degree of integrity.

The passing of my wife has forced me to face the issues I have been avoiding for too long. I now need to take time to reassess who I am and where I stand with regard to these issues. I don't know where this period of retreat and reflection will take me ultimately, but I am certain that this present chapter of life is now over.

I want to express my sincere thanks to you and to everyone who has trusted me and given me the privilege and responsibility of speaking from their pulpits over the years. I would appreciate your understanding at this time and I would be grateful if you did not try to contact me over the coming months. I need to find space to reassess the direction of my life and to discover a new role for the future.

Yours sincerely…

He had said all he wanted to say. There was nothing else to be done other than to despatch the fifty or so emails that had to be sent. When he finally logged out of his computer at around half-past two in the morning, he knew that he had closed a long and important chapter of his life. Nothing would ever be the same again. He wondered how the recipients of his message would react when they opened their mailbox in the morning. For himself, he felt like a solitary traveller, without map or compass, looking out over a vast and featureless wasteland through which he must pass, not knowing his destination, and certain only that the journey would be long and hard.

Next morning he woke around eight o'clock to the smell of bacon and eggs frying in the kitchen. Tim, who was using the guest room they kept for visiting relatives, had been up for some time and had decided that his friend really needed to eat something substantial. Despite Ray's protests that he wasn't hungry, he carried on serving up breakfast for them both.

'It'll do you good,' he said. 'I'm guessing you've got stuff you want to do today. You'll need some energy for that. So eat what you can.'

The two men sat down together. Tim poured two cups of tea and prayed a short blessing over the meal.

'I am a vicar, after all,' he grinned at the end of the prayer. 'Better do things properly for my old mate.'

Ray smiled back at him. People's prayers left him emotionally untouched at the moment, but he valued Tim's friendship and practical help at this time more than he could say. He took a couple of mouthfuls. Having eaten very little for several days, he was actually far hungrier than he'd realised. As he ate, it occurred to him that the last time he'd sat at this table was with the two police officers who'd broken the news of Jean's death. In a couple of days things had changed beyond all recognition. And it was impossible to work out where life would go from here. He was glad that Tim was leaving him to his thoughts and not trying to make small talk.

Neither of them spoke until they'd finished eating. Ray pushed his plate away, poured a second cup of tea. It was as if he needed to say the words in order to strengthen his resolve.

'I'm going to go and see Annie this morning. I've got to sort things out with her before the funeral.'

Ray knew that Tim was sensitive enough not to ask exactly what 'sort things out with her' meant or to offer any advice; he'd learned over the years that there are some things you can help someone with and some things you have to leave them to do on their own. This definitely fell into the latter category.

'Well, I'll be thinking of you and praying for you,' Tim said as he got up and began clearing the table. 'I'll see to what has to be done here. Then I need to go home for a couple of hours. But I'll be back around eight or nine this evening.'

Ray nodded his thanks and left the kitchen. He showered and dressed and tried to prepare himself for a difficult morning.

It was just after eleven o'clock when he arrived at Annie's flat. The door opened as soon as the bell rang, and he knew that she must have been stood in the hallway waiting for him to arrive. With his visit to Edinburgh to see

Ollie and her work in Wales, they hadn't seen each other for ten days and she was obviously eager for his company. Immediately she flung her arms around him. He pushed her away gently but firmly.

'Don't, Annie,' he said. 'Not now. I need to talk to you.'

She reluctantly released her hold and he could see the disappointment and hurt in her eyes. He walked ahead of her into her sitting room and sat down.

'I can't – I mean, I mustn't – stay long. I wanted to see you and tell you what's happening. My head's in a mess and I've got to sort things out. I think I'm going to go away for some time after the funeral.'

She looked at him questioningly.

'What are you saying? I don't want it to be over between us.'

She tried to take hold of his hand, but again he pushed her away.

'I don't know what's going to happen. I don't know what I think about anything any longer – about the future, about us. I just feel so guilty about how I treated Jean, how I lied to her and cheated on her. I don't even know who I am at the moment. Nothing makes sense.'

'I'm sorry too about the way it happened,' she said, lowering her eyes. 'And I'm so sorry about Jean. Maybe we shouldn't have done it the way we did. I'm not proud of all that. But I love you and when this is all over I want to be with you.'

'I know, but I need to be alone for a while.'

'How long will you go away for?'

'I don't know. Two or three months, anyway. Maybe longer. It depends.'

She sensed that his mind was made up and that trying to dissuade him might make things worse.

'If that's what you've got to do, OK, then. But will you keep in touch? At least call me when you get back?'

He gave a non-committal answer and stood up to leave. The tears began to fall down her face and he couldn't resist taking her in his arms.

'Don't make this any harder for me, Annie,' he whispered. 'I love you. But I loved Jean too. And I'll never be able to put right what I did to her. It's tearing me apart and I don't know whether I can trust myself or whether anybody else can ever trust me again. You might be better off without me. Let's just see how things turn out.'

He held her briefly. Then he turned and hurried out of the apartment without daring to glance back.

The day of the funeral was dry and bright and pleasantly warm. It was one of those days in early September when summer is merging gradually into autumn and giving a comforting sense of the year gently moving towards a climax. The kind of day on which cities like Manchester often appear at their best.

Ray and Ollie sat together in the back of the undertaker's limousine as it drove along Barlow Moor Road to the Manchester Crematorium observing an uneasy silence and a fragile truce that was held together only by their mutual grief. The service was scheduled for two o'clock and Ollie had arrived at his parents' home just early enough to allow time to join the other members of the family who were assembled there waiting to travel with the cortège. He and Ray had shared no more than half a dozen words before leaving the house, agreeing to observe the formalities of the occasion for the sake of Jean's memory and their love for her. Not one word passed between them on the short journey.

They had chosen the older of the two chapels because of its greater seating capacity and its facility to relay the service outside. It proved to be a wise choice. Besides the hundred or so people who had taken their places in the chapel, there were at least four or five times that number waiting outside. As they got out of the car, Ray recognised many of those who were standing respectfully in front of the arched entrance to the impressive Victorian edifice – fellow ministers and pastors he'd known for many years, colleagues who'd worked with Jean, neighbours with whom he had little more than a nodding acquaintance but whom she'd got to know and probably helped at some time, even some old school friends of Ollie's who'd enjoyed his mum's home-cooking when they'd come to hang out with him as teenagers. It was an impressive turnout and a clear indication of just how much she was loved and respected.

It was also a painful reminder to Ray of the character of the woman he'd treated so badly and of everything he'd lost so irrevocably. As he walked past these people, he felt as if every eye was boring into him, as if every one of them could see him for what he really was – a calculating hypocrite and a cold-hearted adulterer.

The service was dignified and just different enough from the norm to reflect Jean's warm personality. The coffin was brought in to the sombre strains of the 1928 Hot Five recording of 'West End Blues'. It was the first jazz recording that he'd played for her on one of their early dates, explaining that it came as near to perfection as anything he'd ever heard. 'A bit like you,' he'd often add with a smile. He'd played it so frequently over the years that she'd said to him only half-jokingly, 'You can play that at my funeral and you'll know that wherever I am I'll hear it and think of you.' The hymns were all her favourites – Eleanor Farjeon's 'Morning Has Broken', Graham Kendrick's 'Such Love', and to close the service the stirring music of 'Thine Be the Glory'. Liz, Jean's closest friend since university days, spoke about her quick wit and sense of humour and suggested that it wasn't difficult to see where Ollie had got his talent from. Tim spoke eloquently about the joys of this present life, the blessings of good memories, and the Christian hope for the future. It was, people were heard to say at the end of the service, an uplifting affirmation of faith and a moving tribute to Jean.

For the two men sitting next to each other on the front row, however, it was the bleakest half-hour of their lives. For Ray there was nothing but the burden of his merciless guilt and the barrenness of his unbelieving heart. And for Ollie only a bitter anguish at the loss of his mother and a burning anger at the hypocrisy of his father. They stood side by side for the committal, looking to the rest of the congregation like men united in grief. The truth was very different. As the coffin slid behind the curtain both felt utterly alone and further from each other than they had ever been in their lives. But there were still the conventions of public grief to be observed.

After the benediction had been pronounced, they dutifully made their way together to the side door to take their places on either side of the line of mourners as they left the chapel. They accepted the expressions of sympathy and offered their thanks in response, both of them grateful for the fact that they could put even a little distance between them. When the last of the congregation had filed past, they made their way to the front of the building to mingle with those who had listened to the service from outside, relieved that they could move through the crowd in opposite directions without coming into close contact with each other.

Gradually the crowd began to disperse, leaving only Tim and a dozen of their closest relatives with whom they'd agreed to meet for a meal in a nearby restaurant after the service. As he saw his son coming towards him, Ray's spirits lifted a little. Maybe even now there would be some degree of reconciliation between them. His hopes were quickly dashed.

'I did that for Mum,' Ollie said coldly. 'But it's over between us. I don't want to see you again.'

Before Ray could say anything in reply he turned away, got into his car and drove off. The others were surprised at his sudden departure, unsure of what might have happened. Tim realised the import of that moment and acted quickly to take control. He went over to the little group who were waiting for them and said that he was pretty sure Ray was too exhausted to join them for the meal.

'He's been through such a lot,' he explained. 'Things seem to be just a bit tense between him and Ollie. I think we should probably let him be on his own. I'll take him home. You head on to the restaurant and I'll be with you as soon as I can.'

He came alongside Ray, took his arm and led him to his car.

'Come on, mate. I saw what happened. You don't need to be making conversation at the moment. Let me take you home, then I'll come back and cover for you.'

They said little in the car. Tim suggested when he dropped him off that he'd come back that evening and they could talk properly. Ray agreed and Tim returned to the restaurant as he'd promised. He stayed until the meal had finished and everyone left around six o'clock. They were troubled by Ollie's behaviour at the end of the service, and puzzled by Ray's absence, so he felt he owed it to his friend to allay their concerns by his presence and his carefully edited explanations as best he could.

After that he had to deal with some routine tasks that had been left undone because of his absence from the church for the past few days. By the time he got back it was almost eight o'clock. He opened the door with the key he'd had for the past few days and called out to Ray. There was no answer. He felt a sudden panic. Please God, he thought, don't let it be that he's done something stupid. He rushed up to his room half-expecting to find him laid out on the floor. Ray wasn't there, but the wardrobe door was open and some of his clothes were missing. It was only then that he realised that his car wasn't in the driveway. He must have suddenly decided to leave.

Tim searched the house to see if he'd left a note explaining where he'd gone and what he was intending to do, but after looking for ten minutes he found nothing. He tried calling his mobile, but all he got was the message saying that the person he was trying to contact wasn't available at this time. He sat for a few minutes contemplating this latest turn of events. Then he turned off the lights, locked up the house, and drove home. He wondered if he should inform the police then quickly banished the thought from his mind. It was much too early for that and they'd probably dismiss him as an overzealous do-gooder. Time enough for that kind of action if there was no word in the next twenty-four hours. For now he just hoped and prayed that Ray was alive and safe.

# Nine

## Sanctuary

There was more than one reason why Ollie was determined to leave as quickly as possible after the funeral. For a start, he couldn't bear to be around his dad for a moment longer than necessary. If he never set eyes on the hypocrite again, that would be too soon. And the house had too many memories of his mum. She'd made it home, always warm and welcoming. Now it was just empty and cold. Even being back in Manchester felt all wrong. There was too much that would drag him back into a past he now wanted to escape. He had to get back to Edinburgh. Not because he had a gig to do: the Festival was over and he'd no bookings for a couple of weeks. But he did have a girl to see: Ellen was still very much on his mind and he wanted to talk to her again before it was too late. He'd texted her before he'd left for Manchester, saying only that he had to go home because of a family crisis and that he'd be in touch as soon as he got back. He couldn't bring himself to spell out the words 'My mum is dead'. He wasn't even sure if he could share such devastating news with someone he'd only just met. But now, the more he thought about it, the more he wondered and worried about how she'd have interpreted his brief communication. Would she think he'd just strung her along and dismiss their encounter on the Royal Mile as nothing more than a casual meeting, a chance for him to fill in an empty afternoon and boost his ego by enjoying the company of a pretty girl for an hour or two? He was surprised by the level of his anxiety that Ellen shouldn't think badly of him or of his intentions towards her.

He'd been so anxious to get away that he didn't give a thought as to where he would stay until he was crossing the border into Scotland. The digs he'd been in during the Festival had been basic to say the least. They'd been made tolerable only by the presence of the other lodgers, a couple of fellow comics he knew well, but they would have left by this time. He quickly dismissed the thought of sleeping in his car for two or three nights. His ancient Mini would be a chilly place to spend the hours of darkness, even in September. Apart from that, he didn't feel like roughing it at the moment. There are times when a man needs a little bit of comfort. A quick review of his finances was enough to convince him that he could just about afford to book into a half-decent B&B for ten days, provided he didn't spend too freely in Edinburgh's drinking establishments. He remembered staying at a nice place just outside of the city when he'd done a charity gig there a couple of years before. Charlie and his wife, Agnes, who ran it were great hosts who'd obviously enjoyed having a stand-up comic staying with them. And, for some reason, they'd taken something of a shine to him. When they'd told him he'd always be welcome, they genuinely seemed to mean it. He'd call and make sure they were still running the place. And, if they had a vacancy, that would do him just fine.

That's why at ten o'clock that night he was walking up the path of the walled garden to the front door of the Aberfeldy Guest House in Portobello on the outskirts of Edinburgh. The old stone-built Victorian manse gave an immediate impression of solidity and security that he found comforting, and Charlie's friendly greeting when he answered the door assured him that he was indeed welcome.

'Ollie,' he said stretching out his hand. 'Great to see you again. Lucky we still had a room free. How're you doin', son?'

'Tired and a bit frazzled,' Ollie replied. 'And desperate to sleep.'

Charlie ushered him into a room just off the hallway.

'Aye, ye look shattered. Let me get ye somethin' to eat and drink.'

Ollie gratefully accepted his offer, and when his host went off to the kitchen he dropped his bag on the floor and hung his jacket on the back of the door. The room was spotlessly clean and looked as if it had been furnished by someone who genuinely wanted to make guests feel that they were being invited to stay for a time in someone's home. It felt very different from the kind of characterless motel chains up and down the country where he often spent the night. He closed and bolted the old shutters, and loosened the heavy drapes that framed the window from their ties, allowing them to fall into place. It felt good to be able to shut out the rest of the world and to draw a line under the events of the day.

Charlie returned with a tray that he set down on the sideboard and Ollie muttered his appreciation.

'Ach, ye're welcome, so ye are,' Charlie said as he backed out of the room. 'Ye look as if ye've had a tough day so I'm guessin' ye'll no be wantin' breakfast until nine. I'll gie you a call. Sleep well, son.'

'You got it,' Ollie responded wearily. 'I'll explain in the morning.'

He'd eaten nothing since lunchtime, and he was glad of the toast and tea. He was even more grateful just to be alone in the stillness of the room. His mind was reeling from the events of the day, and the mixture of grief and anger that he'd been suppressing had left him with a headache. He finished his tea, took a couple of paracetamol, got undressed, and fell into bed.

That was the last thing he remembered until he was wakened next morning by a loud banging on the door and the sound of Charlie's voice.

'It's quarter-past nine and if ye don't get up I'll be eatin' yer breakfast masel!'

Ollie roused himself, pulled on his clothes quickly and went through to the dining room. The other guests had gone by that time, and Agnes greeted him with a hug while Charlie brought in his breakfast from the kitchen and set it in front of him. It was the same splendid 'full Scottish' that he'd enjoyed so much on his last visit, though he recalled ruefully that the last time he'd sat down to this kind of fare was on his ill-fated meeting with his dad a few weeks earlier. Despite that unhappy memory, he quickly devoured the food in front of him. And the effects of a good night's sleep, a hearty breakfast, and the sanctuary of a place where his hosts' only concern at that time was to look after their guest all combined to make him feel better than he'd done for many days.

Agnes brought him a second pot of tea and pulled up a chair opposite him. She folded her arms and looked straight at him in a way that gave him the feeling that she understood there must be a particular reason for his visit. Her university education and the time she'd spent in the teaching profession had ironed out the strong Glaswegian accent she'd once shared with her husband.

'Well, this is an unexpected pleasure, seeing you, Ollie. Tell me how you're doing.'

He took a sip of his tea before replying.

'I'm OK. Well… sort of OK.'

He paused again for a moment or two. Charlie joined them from the kitchen with a tea towel still over his arm, and sat down beside his wife. Years of serving people and listening to their stories had made them as alert and sensitive as any trained counsellors to the nuances of a conversation and the need to listen without interrupting. So they sat and waited until Ollie felt ready to speak.

'My mum was killed in a road accident and the funeral was yesterday. So, you know…'

'Oh, Ollie, I'm really sorry,' Agnes said.

She pulled her chair round closer to him and put her arm lightly on his shoulder. It was a simple gesture, not in any way extravagant or unduly emotional. But it had a kind of unaffected motherly quality that Ollie appreciated.

'Yeah, it is hard. And it's complicated. There's other stuff going on that I can't really talk about.'

Agnes took her hand off his shoulder and drew it down his arm.

'That's fine, son. Don't say any more than you want to. Your room's available for the next couple of weeks if you want to stay.'

'I'd appreciate that. There's a girl I met when I was up at the Festival and I want to see her again.'

Charlie obviously saw the opportunity to lighten the conversation and move away from the difficult subject they'd touched on.

'O aye... So that's it. You've found yersel a lassie. I might ha' known ye were up to something.'

Agnes lowered her eyebrows and gave her husband a nudge.

'Stop it, Charlie. You'll embarrass the boy. Come on, there's work to be done in the kitchen. Let Ollie get on with his day.'

They went back into the kitchen, leaving Ollie to finish his tea. He sent a text message to Ellen:

> Back in Auld Reekie. Can we meet soon plse? I'll explain my absence.

As soon as he'd written it, he considered adding a bit more, maybe say that he'd missed her. But he quickly decided that might be a bit premature given that they'd only really met once. Better to keep it brief. As soon as he'd pressed the send button, he wondered how she might react. Would she reply or just ignore his message? Maybe he was putting too much hope on a one-off chance meeting. That was certainly a possibility, but not one he wanted to contemplate for long. He resolved to do something to keep himself occupied for what was left of the morning and clear his mind of such unwanted thoughts. The sun was shining, it was a warm day, and the guesthouse was less than five minutes from the seafront. A walk would be just right and keep him from worrying too much about whether or not Ellen would respond to his text message. He showered and dressed quickly and headed to the beach.

He'd never had time or inclination to walk there on his previous visit to Portobello and he was pleasantly surprised to find that the promenade, which ran alongside the beach for a couple of miles, was unspoiled and entirely bereft of the usual amusement arcades and tacky souvenir shops. He certainly didn't feel like that kind of enforced jollity today. There were very few other people around and, apart from the occasional pub or café, there was nothing that would offer the kind of entertainment that would draw the typical weekend pleasure-seeker. Clearly the good burghers of Portobello had no interest in attracting the hedonistic masses to their town. Blackpool it certainly was not! For the first time since he'd headed south in response to his dad's phone call, his mind slotted back into familiar stand-up mode, and he began to mull over the comic possibilities of exploring the contrast between the two towns. He'd just reached into his jacket pocket to pull out the little notebook in which he scribbled down ideas when his phone bleeped. A text. He stood still, took a deep breath, and opened the message. It was from Ellen!

Glad ur back. Missed u. Hope ur OK. Where r u now?

A wave of relief and happiness swept over him. His fingers felt fat and clumsy as he fumbled with the keyboard attempting to send a quick response.

Walking on P'bello prom. Staying at a B&B here.

The reply came back within seconds. Ellen was obviously much more adept at texting than he was!

U want 2 have lunch? I'll pay this time! Gt little restaurant just off prom – Zucchini Rendezvous – I can book a table and mt u there in 40 mins.

He wasn't about to turn down an invitation like that.

Great. Thanks. See you there

Ellen, it seemed, was as keen to meet up again as he was. It was better than he dared to hope.

Ollie slipped his phone back in his pocket and, with time to kill, he sat on the promenade wall for the next quarter of an hour, looking out over the Firth of Forth and trying to take stock of all that had happened in the last couple of weeks. The darkness of betrayal and bereavement still hung heavily over him, but deep inside there was a hint of light, like the first glimmer of a breaking dawn after a long night. It felt good and his spirits began to lift. On a whim, he kicked off his shoes, pulled off his socks and stuffed them in his pocket, and began to stroll along the beach. Though he could not completely shake off the feeling of loss, as he walked barefooted through the sand and looked out across the expanse of water he had an uplifting sense of the larger ongoing reality of a universe in which our individual lives are played out for only a brief moment of time. It seemed to offer some consolation even if he couldn't put into words just why that was.

A brief exchange of words with an elderly man out exercising his dog confirmed that he was heading in the right direction for the restaurant. 'On the first side street you'll come to. No more than ten minutes away,' he told Ollie. It occurred to him that he should get there early and be waiting for Ellen when she arrived. So he made his way back to the promenade, put his shoes and socks back on, and set off at a brisk pace. The prospect of seeing Ellen again brought a smile to his face.

When he reached the restaurant, he could see immediately why it would be a favourite of hers. It gave that same impression of unpretentious self-confidence that he'd noticed in her, a kind of what-you-see-is-what-you-get attitude that made you feel this was a person or a place you could trust. The bright orange blinds and signage and the light grey paintwork that framed its large picture windows caused it to stand out cheerfully against the reddish-brown sandstone of the three-storey terraced building in which it occupied the ground floor. A glance through the window revealed the functional furnishings that you tend to find in family-run eating-houses where good food and pleasant company matter more than trendy designer-coordinated décor. The inexpensive but interesting menu and the appetising aroma wafting from the open kitchen combined to stimulate the appetite even of a man who'd eaten a breakfast as substantial as Ollie had enjoyed just a couple of hours before.

He was engrossed in reading the menu in the window and savouring the prospect of the penne arrabiata served with garlic bread when he heard someone calling his name. He turned to see a smiling young woman wearing white jeans and a denim jacket hurrying towards him. The possibility that he might be a little disappointed on meeting Ellen again had fleetingly crossed his mind that morning. He'd heard one of his mates talk about the 'second date syndrome' – the realisation that what you imagined to be a genuine attraction was in reality no more than a passing fancy that quickly fades in the cold light of day. But that thought was instantly dispelled at the sight of the fair-skinned, copper-haired girl standing in front of him now. She was every bit as attractive as he remembered, and more. She gave him a hug that demonstrated the same natural, uninhibited approach to life that he'd noticed in her easy laughter when he'd first spotted her at his lunchtime gig in The Pipers' Kitchen.

'It's great to see you again,' he said. 'I was a bit worried you might think that I'd just left town and was just fobbing you off with a story.'

She looked at him with an expression that suggested her response was half-serious.

'Well, to tell you the truth, I *did* wonder if you'd just taken advantage of my youth and innocence. So I was really pleased to get your message saying you were back. But what are you doing out here in Portobello? I had you down as a boy for the bright lights of the city.'

He related how he'd stayed at the Aberfeldy Guest House before and how Charlie and Agnes had made him feel at home.

'And besides that,' he added as they stepped into the restaurant, 'I needed somewhere just to be quiet for a day or two. I'll tell you the story over lunch.'

They chose a table tucked in a little corner by the window which would allow them to chat without being overheard, and when they'd ordered their meal, Ollie explained the circumstances behind his sudden departure. Ellen listened intently without interrupting until he'd finished.

'Oh, I'm really sorry,' she said sympathetically. 'That's terrible.'

'And I'm sorry I didn't say more in my text message or contact you from Manchester,' he apologised. 'It was difficult. I was staying with one of my mates and I couldn't get my head straight to do anything. I was quite close to my mum and it was a big shock.'

'So you didn't stay at home with your dad?' she asked.

Ollie immediately felt annoyed with himself for opening the door to that question. It was the subject he'd hoped to avoid at all costs.

'Well...' He paused for a moment, trying to find the right words and to say as little as possible '... let's just say that we don't get on too well. There's a lot of stuff... best not to talk about that.'

There was a momentary uncomfortable hiatus in the conversation, and it was a relief to them both when the waiter arrived carrying their food. He recognised Ellen from previous visits and made some teasing comments about the amount of free time students had these days. Her good-natured response and ready laughter quickly eased the slight tension that had been caused by Ollie's obvious discomfort at her question about his dad.

The rest of their lunch passed without any further awkward moments. The pleasure of Ellen's company was sufficient to distract Ollie's mind from his sense of grief and over coffee they chatted happily about the bookings Ollie had lined up for the next few months and the coming semester of Ellen's final year at university. Despite his protests, she insisted on paying the bill as she'd promised.

'Well, I'm a working woman,' she said with a grin as they walked back along the promenade. 'There are still enough soft-hearted tourists in the city who'll take pity on an attractive tour guide trying to earn an honest penny.'

Before they turned up to the main road where she could catch a bus back into the city, they sat together on the same bit of the promenade wall where Olllie had stopped on his way to meet her. If he hadn't been so nervous of appearing too eager and scaring her off, he would have kissed her at that point. He was uncharacteristically anxious to 'do the right thing' and make a good impression. Living an itinerant life and having all the normal passions of a young male of his age, he hadn't always been held back by such scruples in his relationships with the opposite sex. But this was altogether different from the casual encounters which were part and parcel of life on the road in his particular line of work. *She* was different, and *his feelings* were different to anything he'd experienced before.

He was conscious of the fact that in just over a week he'd need leave for his next gig and he wanted to tell her how he felt. Sitting in the afternoon sun looking out over the beach, this seemed like just the right moment. He turned to face her and gave a nervous cough as he tried to clear his throat.

'You sound as if you're about to deliver a speech,' she said laughing at his obvious discomfort. 'Surely you're not *nervous* – you're used to bigger audiences than just me!'

'Well, I *am* – about to make a speech, that is. And I *am* a bit nervous as well.'

She realised he was being serious and it took her aback. It's got to be something important, she thought to herself, when a stand-up comic makes a serious speech. Ollie could see her discomfort and reached across and touched her hand lightly and tentatively.

'Look, I know we've only met a couple of times and… well… we hardly know each other. But I need to tell you that I really like you – like you a lot. I'd love this to be something more than just a passing thing. I'd like us to get to know each other… *properly*.'

He was aware that he was struggling for the right words and afraid he might have messed it up. He was trying to think of something else to say that would round it off appropriately. But Ellen leaned over and kissed him on the cheek.

'OK,' she said without any fuss. 'I'd really like that too. Now I need to catch my bus. I've got a crowd of eager tourists waiting to give me their hard-earned cash.'

She stood up and slipped her hand into his, and that simple act aroused in him a feeling of deep contentment. Other than agreeing to meet the following evening, they hardly spoke a word as they walked hand in hand to the bus stop. With other girls who'd responded to his overtures, Ollie had always had a sense of male pride in making another conquest. Sometimes, to his shame, he'd even found himself thinking of ways to work the encounter into his stand-up routine. Now, if he'd been able to put his thoughts into words, he would simply have said, 'It feels like I'm in a really safe place for the first time in a very long time.'

# Ten

## Running Away

By the time Ray got home from the funeral he'd already decided to leave as quickly as possible. Of course, he felt bad about running out on Tim who'd been a tremendous help, but he knew he'd reached the end of his tether and he hoped his friend would somehow understand. He had to get away – away from everything and everyone. His life was mess, a horrible sordid mess, and he didn't have a clue how to sort it out. The truth was, he admitted to himself, he didn't have a clue about anything any longer. Nothing made sense. His wife was dead, his son hated him, his ministry was at an end, his life had fallen apart. The house was no longer home. It was a mausoleum, a burial chamber for everything he'd believed and held dear. He didn't belong here. He didn't belong anywhere. Tim might come back at any time and he didn't want to be around and have to explain things. So he quickly grabbed some toiletries from the bathroom, shoved some clothes into a bag and hurried out of the house.

He pulled out of the driveway without making any conscious decision as to where he was heading. His only aim was to get away as far and as fast as possible. It wasn't until he saw the sign for the Knutsford Services that he fully realised he was heading south on the motorway. A sudden and almost irresistible urge came over him to come off at the next exit, drive round the roundabout, and head back on the north-bound carriageway. The solution to all his problems could be just a few miles up the road. One sharp pull on the steering wheel is all it would take. He could end his life on the same stretch of road where Jean had died. At least it would give some kind of symmetry to what was an otherwise senseless tragedy. The pain would stop, the shame and guilt would sink into a sea of oblivion. It was a crazy thought, the product of his emotional exhaustion and spiritual desolation. *He knew that.* But it had a dark and alluring beauty that drew him deathwards like the enchanting music of the Sirens in the ancient myths. And, like Odysseus blocking the ears of his crew with beeswax and lashing himself to the mast, he turned the car radio on loudly, gripped the steering wheel tightly, and kept his foot hard down on the accelerator until junction 18 of the M6 was lost in his rear-view mirror.

It was only after he'd driven about 100 miles and found himself on the M40 that the truth surfaced from his subconscious mind. *He was heading for Bournemouth* – the place where Jean had grown up, where she had taken him to visit her folks a few months after they'd met, where they'd got married, where they'd spent so many summer holidays as a family. The place from which she'd started her last journey northwards just a couple of weeks ago. Other than the fact that he wanted to make sure he avoided any contact with her sister and her husband, he'd no clear idea of what he'd do when he got there. *He just needed to go to Bournemouth.* A few moments ago he'd been driving with no notion of where he was heading. Now the thought was lodged in his mind, as jagged and hard-edged as a splinter of broken glass stuck in his finger. It sharpened his senses, forcing him to the realisation that he was hungry and thirsty and needed to eat and drink if he was to complete the journey. He stopped at the Warwick Services just long enough to fill up with petrol and pick up a sandwich and coffee before getting back on to the motorway. He was resolved not to stop again until he reached the south coast.

Twenty miles further down the road, as the late afternoon passed into evening, he stretched over and flipped open the glove compartment. Jean had told him more than once that it wasn't safe to do it while he was driving, but he'd done it so often, he always told her, that he never needed to take his eyes off the road. His fingers instinctively knew where to find what he was looking for, and he took hold of the CD on the top of the pile, flicked open the box with one hand, removed the disc and slipped it into the player.

*Kind of Blue* was the album he played whenever the world seemed a tough place, whenever he was weary or confused or ill at ease with life. It never failed to weave its spell over him. The laid-back, languid entry of the piano and bass in the opening bars always evoked for him a sense of wide-open spaces and unbroken vistas, of long lonely walks on cool spring evenings, of the gentle melancholy of a lingering dusk morphing into the quiet anticipation of an advancing dawn that would gradually penetrate the shadows of night. Then the passage that always quickened his pulse – the bass riff, picking up the rhythm and summoning the percussion and the horns before giving way to the glorious breathy trumpet of Miles Davis. It was a sound – though 'sound' always seemed an utterly inadequate word for it – that carried him beyond the narrow boundary of his feeble thoughts and into a realm that transcended words and logic. A realm where there was no right or wrong, no good or bad, no past or future. A realm of pure sound in which only consciousness existed untroubled by the hard realities of life. Even the title of that first track touched him deeply. Just those two simple one-syllable words: 'So What'. It was the question he'd been asking in one way or another all his life. And this evening of all evenings, they perfectly articulated his reaction to all that had happened. So what? So what does it *mean*? So what does it *matter*? So what can be *done*? So what do I *care*? So what...

He was enough of a jazz buff to be able to discuss the extravagant leap forward represented by the music on this album, and he could talk for an hour on Davis' creative reaction against the often frenetic improvisations and breakneck tempos of the hard bop of Charlie Parker and Dizzy Gillespie in the 1940s. He'd even once attempted to give a talk, though with embarrassingly limited success, to a group of church organists on 'modal jazz', explaining how Davis and some of his contemporaries had broken through the limitations of allowing the chord progressions to dictate where the music went and moved into a freer kind of improvisation that was based on the notes in a series of scales or 'modes'. Most of his hearers had looked at him with bemused expressions until he played a track for them and the flowing melodic lines had invoked a modicum of appreciation even in such an initially unresponsive audience.

Jean had often teased him about his efforts to share his passion with others, but the truth was that jazz, and particularly the music of Miles Davis, had become for him something much more important than an intellectual appreciation of the technicalities of improvisation or even an aesthetic pleasure in the music itself. It had become a kind of metaphor for life, or at least what he wished life could be. Whereas most of his colleagues in the Church would have had a scripture text or a quote from one of the great theologians on display in their study, he had handwritten some words onto a piece of paper and stuck them to the wall above his desk. It was a reply he'd once made to a friend who confessed himself to be completely puzzled by the freer form of jazz that Davis played and that he loved so much. It had become a kind of mantra for Ray:

The point is to sing your own song,
The chords are there to help you, not to hold you back
So sing it with abandon
Just be sure you're true to the music,
And somehow or other you'll find your way home.

It was an ideal that both inspired him and also burdened him with a constant feeling of disappointment at his inability to find his 'own song'. He'd never had a crisis of belief in the sense in which many people understood that phrase, never *rejected* his faith. Rather, he had a growing sense that he had never really *discovered* it. He knew its chords – the historical events in which its story was rooted, the theological reflections and doctrines by which its truths could be articulated and communicated, the liturgical practices in which the Church dramatised and acted out its faith, the practical community projects through which believers served others – and they provided the framework on which the rhythms of his life were based. But the soaring melodies of the spirit that echoed through the ages and moved the souls of the saints and mystics – of those he knew little if anything. As a consequence, the lyrics he was singing were jaded and second-hand, and he felt increasingly that he was attempting to sing them to a melody whose notes he could no longer hear and could only dimly recall.

As he drove ever southwards and the music that he'd loved so much for so long continued to play, a profound sadness threatened to overwhelm him. He was forced to a depressing conclusion. *He could never be free.* He could never be free for he no longer had any idea 'where home is'. That was certainly true spiritually. He had nothing that he could describe as faith at that moment, he had severed the links with his ministry, and he could see no place for him in the Church in the future. And it was no less true in literal terms. Manchester, where he'd lived for twenty-five years, was a city from which he'd just fled, leaving behind all he'd known for the greater part of his adult life. His house, the home he'd shared with Jean, was a place to which he could never return. Now he was heading for Bournemouth because... He couldn't complete that sentence. Why *was* he heading there? It was a place full of memories, but the last thing he wanted to do was to try to recapture the past. So why? A thought began gradually to form in his mind, vague and ill-defined at first, but increasingly clearer and sharper as he reached the outskirts of the town. The point of this visit was not to retrace his steps and definitely not to wallow in nostalgia. It was, to use a phrase he'd long hated, all about bringing some closure to things. He was going to Bournemouth to write an ending. An ending of a chapter? Certainly. The ending of the story? Perhaps...

It was getting on for eleven o'clock when he reached Boscombe near to where Jean's parents had lived when they first met, and parked his car in a side street without pausing to check if there were any parking restrictions. His first thought when he stepped out of the car, despite the lateness of the hour, was to get to the beach. He set off walking briskly in the direction to the pier. As he made the steady descent down Sea Road, he thought of the walks that he and Jean had taken hand in hand so many times in the early morning sunshine, chatting contentedly as they anticipated a long summer's day to be spent on the beach. That all seemed a very long time ago now. A few end-of-season holidaymakers passed him heading in the opposite direction to their hotels and guest houses for the night. He hadn't booked any accommodation. But oddly enough, for a man who loved home comforts and always appreciated a warm bed, it didn't trouble him at all.

When he reached the pier, he stood for a while, leaning on the rail by the steps that led down to the beach and listening to the sound of the waves lapping on the shore. The heavy sadness that he'd felt earlier in the car engulfed him again and he began to mutter to himself some lines he remembered from 'Dover Beach'. Matthew Arnold's poem was one of the set texts for English in his last year at school. As a teenager it had been nothing more than a mildly interesting piece of English literature. He'd rediscovered it only in the last couple of years and he'd found himself turning to it frequently. He'd never intentionally set out to commit it to memory, but to his surprise he'd discovered that he could actually recall most of the lines. He must have read it even more often than he'd thought in the last few months. As he mouthed the words quietly to himself, they sounded to him now like an epitaph for his life.

> The Sea of Faith
> Was once, too, at the full, and round earth's shore
> Lay like the folds of a bright girdle furled.
> But now I only hear
> Its melancholy, long, withdrawing roar,
> Retreating, to the breath
> Of the night-wind, down the vast edges drear
> And naked shingles of the world …

When he was seventeen years old 'the vast edges drear and naked shingles of the world' had seemed an odd figure of speech. Now more than thirty years later they perfectly expressed the loneliness and desolation of this moment.

He suddenly became aware that a police car had pulled up slowly beside him. He'd been too distracted to notice that the occupants had been watching him for several minutes. The young officer in the passenger seat stepped out and looked at him warily, uncertain what approach to take. Middle-aged men with tear-stained faces mumbling poetry were certainly not typical of the problems he normally encountered on the beach at night.

'Are you all right, sir?' he asked with a quizzical expression.

'I'm fine,' Ray replied hesitantly. 'Just taking a breath of air before I head home.'

'Home? You *have* got somewhere to stay?'

'Oh, yes,' Ray lied. 'I'm visiting my wife's family in Boscombe for a couple of days.'

'And what's your name, sir?

'My name… I'm Ray Young.'

For a fleeting moment he imagined he saw a flicker of recognition in his questioner's eyes. But the policeman continued with his interrogation in the same detached professional manner.

'Are you on your own?' he asked.

'Yes. Just thought I'd enjoy the sea breezes before I turn in for the night.'

Ray hoped he was managing to sound cheerful, or at least reasonably normal.

The policeman didn't seem entirely convinced, but recognising that the man standing in front of him was clean and tidy and showed no sign of having drunk too much or of being likely to cause any trouble, he decided to give him the benefit of the doubt.

'Well, just be careful. It's getting late. I'd head home now, if I were you. Goodnight, sir.'

He hesitated briefly before joining his colleague back in the car. They drove off leaving Ray alone again with his melancholy thoughts and the 'long, withdrawing roar' of the receding tide.

The distance from Boscombe Pier to Bournemouth Pier was less than a mile and a half. Every year when they'd come on holiday he and Jean would regularly run or walk from one to the other in the afternoon before they went back home to freshen up and meet friends for an evening meal. Tonight he had nowhere to go, no one to meet, and nothing to look forward to. Tonight he would make the walk on his own. He wiped his eyes with the backs of his hands, and then thrust his hands into his pockets to dry them, just as he used to do as a child. He stood for a moment, sighed deeply and set off for the distant pier. Even before he'd gone 100 yards he knew that there was something forming in his mind, something he was afraid to articulate but could not ignore, something he would have to face before he completed the distance. It wasn't so much a thought or an idea. More a dark half-shapen form lurking in the shadows of his consciousness. And as he walked, it began to come into sharper focus and to take on substance until he understood with a startlingly unemotional clarity the reason for his trip to Bournemouth and the purpose of this walk by the sea. The destination to which he was travelling was at once far further and yet much nearer than the pier. He still did not dare to put it into words, but he knew what he had to do to reach the final stage of his journey, and he was determined to do it calmly and deliberately.

He'd walked just over half a mile when he stopped, quickly removed his shoes and socks, and tucked them neatly under a bench where he thought no one was likely to fall over them. Odd, he thought to himself, how you think about something like that at a moment like this.

Then, without any hesitation, he went down the five or six steps that led to the beach. The sand felt cool and damp beneath his feet. It was a soothing sensation after such a long and emotionally exhausting day, and he was tempted to linger. But he knew that he dare not delay. By a sheer act of will he forced himself to stride purposefully onward to the water's edge, where he took off his clothes, laid them in a neat pile and walked into the sea. He didn't stop until the water rose above his chest and he could taste the saltwater as it slapped into his face. His rational mind was telling him that he still had time to make a choice. He could turn back to the shore, dry himself off quickly, get dressed, and try to find himself a decent B&B. Or he could allow the sea to carry him wherever it would. Whether it was from the sudden chill of the water or the surge of fear that ran through him, he began to shiver uncontrollably. He felt alone and vulnerable, at the mercy of the sea, an orphaned child in a pitiless and uncaring universe. But he would not permit himself to falter. There could be no going back. Not to the life he'd been living for so long. Easing his feet off the bottom, he let the water take his weight and began to swim out to the open sea and into the heart of the darkness.

# Eleven

## No Escape

There was a Light and a Voice. Dim and faint, and far away at first. The Light and the Voice penetrated only the outer edges of his consciousness. They were reaching out to him from a reality he'd left behind and he tried to ignore them. In a moment they would stop. Everything would stop. There would be absolute quiet and total darkness. But the Light kept shining and the Voice continued to call. The Voice was closer and louder, more persistent, calling his name over and over. And it was coming from someone very near to him now, someone who got under him and grabbed hold of him, someone who could bear his weight, someone who turned him onto his back and swam to the shore with him.

'Stay with me, Ray,' the Voice said. 'I've got you. Stay with me...'

He'd heard the Voice somewhere before, but it was impossible to recall whose it was or where he'd heard it. He slipped back into the darkness again until the scraping of the gritty sand on his heels dragged him unwillingly back into semi-consciousness. And someone else was there helping the Voice. Someone else took hold of him and pulled him out of the water, turned him on to his front, slapped him on the back, encouraged him to cough. And the Light was there too, but brighter, much brighter. Blinding him, causing him to squint. He struggled to stand, but a wave of nausea came over him. He felt himself slipping back into the darkness, and the Voice and the Light faded back into the distance.

He knew nothing after that until he woke to find himself in a hospital ward. The sun was streaming through the window by his bed and a nurse was standing over him smiling reassuringly and speaking softly.

'How are you feeling, Mr Young? You're in the Royal Bournemouth Hospital. You were brought in late last night. You've been asleep for a long time.'

It took a few moments to muster his thoughts into some kind of order. The previous day's events drifted gradually into focus. The funeral, escaping from Manchester, the long drive south, arriving in Bournemouth, walking along the prom… But what happened after that was hazy and ill-defined. He could recall the chill of the water and an all-consuming urge to get as far out to sea as he could. But what he couldn't work out now was why that had mattered so much to him. What was in his mind when he walked into the sea? Did he want to die? Was he trying to escape? Or was he just tempting fate, testing providence, trying to make something – *anything* – happen that would ease the pain? He could find no answers to those questions. And he'd no idea what had happened after that or how he'd got here. There was a touch on his arm and the nurse spoke to him again.

'Can you hear me, Ray? You've had a bit of a shock. You were exhausted when you came in last night. The doctor will be here to see you in an hour or so.'

'I'm OK,' he mumbled. 'But how did I get here?'

She turned and beckoned to a dark-haired young man wearing navy blue trousers and a casual top. Ray hadn't noticed him standing at the foot of the bed.

'Well, here's your answer, right on cue,' she said, beckoning to the visitor to sit down beside the bed.

'This is Constable Eric Bradley. I think he'll be able to explain things. If you feel strong enough, I'll leave you two to chat. But just for a few moments. You still need to rest.'

Ray couldn't think why the man sitting by his bed looked vaguely familiar until he began to speak. Immediately he recognised the voice as that of the young police officer who'd spoken to him when he was standing by Boscombe Pier.

'Mr Young. Good to see you looking so much better than you did last night. How much can you remember about what happened?'

'Not much,' Ray admitted. 'And I've no idea how I ended up here in hospital.'

He tried to get himself into a sitting position, only to discover that his body ached all over. His visitor helped to prop him up on his pillow and drew his chair close so that Ray could hear him without difficulty.

'Let me fill you in. For some reason, I couldn't get you out of my mind after we spoke last night. I had a feeling that something might be wrong and I persuaded my colleague to drive back along Undercliff Drive to check that you were all right. We drove along the prom, and when we couldn't find you there I decided to get out of the car and take a look on the beach. Fortunately we stopped at the right spot and I discovered your clothes by the edge of the water.'

Ray began to worry that he might have to answer some uncomfortable questions. Better to say something that would cut off such enquiries.

'I just had one of those crazy notions that middle-aged men sometimes get. Decided to go for a moonlight swim. I must have been more tired than I realised.'

Constable Bradley looked less than convinced by this explanation. But he let it pass without comment and went on with his account of the previous night's events.

'We got a searchlight out of the car and spotted you well out to sea. We could see you were struggling. I'm a decent swimmer, so I stripped off and got into the water. By the time I got to you, you were in some distress. A few minutes later and you'd have been in real trouble. We called an ambulance and they got you here quickly. You weren't in any state to answer questions or give us any details about yourself. But we checked your wallet and found your driving licence. We got some numbers from your mobile phone, too. I couldn't get hold of your son, but I did manage to speak to the Reverend Tim Johnson this morning before I finished my shift. He told me about your wife's death and the funeral yesterday. You drove a long way after what had to be an emotionally demanding day. You must have been exhausted even before you got into the sea.'

He paused and looked at Ray with an expression that indicated an anxiety that went beyond merely professional concern.

'I'm sure the hospital will arrange for people more qualified than I am in counselling to speak with you. But I just wanted to come in this morning when I finished my shift and let you know what happened.'

Ray reached out to shake hands.

'It seems I owe you a debt of gratitude, Constable Bradley. You've probably saved my life. Though I guess you'll say that you were just doing your duty.'

The young police officer gripped Ray's hand warmly and held it for a moment or two before he spoke again.

'Well, normally that's exactly what I would say. But in this case it was more than that. I didn't immediately recognise you last night, even after you told me your name. It was only after I got back into the car that it dawned on me – who I'd just been talking to. You wouldn't remember it, I'm sure, but we've actually met before. A couple of years ago you were the guest speaker at a conference at the church I attend. You spoke about being a follower of Jesus beyond the walls of the church, about the difference faith should make to our everyday life. It made a big impression on me and I spoke to you at the end of one of the sessions. You were really helpful. In fact, you prayed for me. To be honest, you've been something of a hero for me ever since. As soon as I realised you were *that* Ray Young, I had to come back. I had a really strong sense that something was wrong…'

He hesitated for a second or two before adding, 'I just think it was a God thing that I met you last night.'

Just to know that the man who was sitting by your bedside had saved your life would have been enough in itself to make a man emotional. Given the postscript he had just added to his story, the impact of his presence and his words on Ray were all the greater, and he struggled to reply. His words came in fits and starts as he fought back the tears.

'You're very kind… but you need to know… I'm no hero… far from it. My life's in a mess… I've lost everything… my wife, my son, my ministry… I don't know what I believe any longer… I don't know why I went into the sea last night… I'm scared to think about it…'

Eric Bradley had been confronted with grief often enough in his career in the police force to know when well-intentioned words could be unhelpful. He resisted the temptation to add to what he'd already said and allowed Ray time to compose himself and draw their conversation to a conclusion.

'I really appreciate what you've done. Especially taking the time to come in to see me now. I guess you'd better just keep praying for me. It might do some good.'

'I'll certainly do that, I promise you,' his visitor replied. 'And I'm sure my pastor would be very glad to speak with you, if you'd like that. But I'd better go now and get some sleep. I'm on duty again tonight. And if you don't mind, I'll call back in to see you.'

They shook hands again and he left, leaving Ray to reflect on his visit, with its unexpected revelation of an earlier meeting, and his rescuer's conviction that he'd returned to the beach last night in response to a divine prompting. There was a time he would have agreed that such things were more than mere coincidence. Now he was much less sure. And much less comfortable with the thought that God, if indeed he existed, was on his case and in close pursuit. Just as it had done yesterday after the funeral, the same desperate urge to escape took possession of him again.

By two o'clock in the afternoon he was back behind the wheel of his car. The doctor who'd spoken with him later that morning had assured him that there appeared to be no lasting physical damage from his ordeal the night before. However, he thought it best that his patient should remain in hospital for a couple of days, 'just to check out some things... make sure you're OK'. From the manner in which he offered this opinion, Ray suspected that it was an oblique reference to a session with a psychiatrist, a prospect he dreaded. He'd also begun to worry that he might be the recipient of visits and the offer of pastoral care from the church Constable Bradley attended. He knew he couldn't cope with that. All he wanted was to get away from everything and everybody who would remind him of who he had been and who might try to fix him and restore him to his former way of life. So, despite the protests of the doctor, he'd insisted on checking himself out of hospital and taking a taxi back to where he'd parked his car. A day before he'd wanted more than anything to get to Bournemouth. Now the only thing he wanted was to get away as quickly as possible.

On his way out of town he stopped to fill up with petrol. As he was waiting in the queue to pay, he overheard an elderly couple in front of him chatting enthusiastically about the delights of their visit to the New Forest. It was a pleasant autumn afternoon and the thought of a more peaceful rural setting seemed as attractive a prospect as anything could be at this time. In less than an hour he'd parked the car and was walking slowly in a part of the forest where there were few other people around. The relative solitude, the touch on his skin of the soft breeze, the sight of the ponies grazing on the open heathland, all combined to make him feel, if not better, at least a little less on edge than he'd been for many days. He knew the region and its history well enough from previous visits to be aware of the irony of the name. Almost a thousand years had passed since William the First had flagrantly displaced the commoners living in the surrounding hamlets to create a royal forest where he could enjoy the pleasures of deer hunting undisturbed. Yet succeeding generations had continued to call it the *New* Forest. He took some consolation from that. Compared to the slow progress of history and the unhurried processes of nature, we're all just 'passing through'. And passing through briefly, at that. It didn't change things or remove his problems. However, it did serve to remind him that, one way or another, they'd come to an end one day. Cold consolation, but enough to keep him going. And for that small mercy he was grateful.

He drove to Beaulieu, a village to which he and Jean had come most years when on holiday in Bournemouth, and wandered along the cobbled High Street. She'd adored the olde-worlde charm of the place with its buildings dating from the sixteenth century, and would sometimes tease him that she'd love to retire to a village like this. That thought, and the realisation that retirement was for ever denied to her, brought a stab of regret that cut him to the heart, and he tried to brace himself against it. He kept walking until he reached the quaintly named Ye Olde Bakery Tea Room. The first time they'd seen it, the ill-considered pastiche of the name had made them laugh, but afternoon tea there had always been a must in their excursions into the New Forest. He stood outside looking at the red-brick building remembering a very different time when life had been much simpler and the future had appeared much brighter. And now, for the first time, he stepped inside alone and sat at a table by himself.

It was disconcerting: despite all that had happened in his life, the room was unchanged from their last visit. White-washed brickwork contrasted with the lead-black of the old baking ovens set into the walls, and the white cotton tablecloths were laid ready for the ritual of afternoon tea. At three of the tables white-haired couples conversed in subdued, confidential tones. The only other sound was the chink of china cups on saucers. It was as if time had stood still here while the world outside, or at least that part of it in which Ray lived, had changed beyond all recognition for ever. A waitress in a black dress with a white starched apron came to take his order. She tried to make pleasant small talk, asking him if he was on holiday and if he'd visited the New Forest before. But Ray was anxious to avoid giving answers that might reveal the true reason for his visit to a stranger and told her only the half-truth that he was passing through on 'a kind of business trip'.

In less than ten minutes she had set his sandwiches and cakes in front of him and left him alone with his thoughts. He ate slowly, allowing his mind to go over what had happened to him in the last twenty-four hours. He'd always considered himself to be the kind of person who could cope with pressure and disappointment. He could get as frustrated as the next man when things went wrong, and he had his occasional dark days. But throughout his adult life and ministry, when colleagues had sought counselling or taken time out to go on retreat, he'd felt grateful for his mental resilience and emotional resources that enabled him to deal with difficult circumstances and negative emotions. He could never imagine himself completely unable to cope or having to ask someone else for help. So why had he left Manchester without a word to anyone? And what was he to make of last night? He hadn't set off from the shore completely resolved to die. *So what was he doing* – heading out to sea in the pitch darkness, pushing himself far beyond his physical strength, going to a distance and depth that he knew were too much for his limited capability as a swimmer? Sitting in the safety and comfort of a cosy, country tearoom, he faced the truth that he could no longer evade: *It wasn't so much that he wanted to die. Rather, he'd reached a point where he no longer wanted to live. He was trying to escape from life.*

He must have been sitting for a while without eating or drinking, allowing the significance of that realisation to sink in when he became aware of someone speaking to him.

'Is everything all right, sir? You've been sitting very still and we wondered if you might be feeling unwell.'

He looked up to see the waitress standing by his table. She had an expression of genuine anxiety that touched him deeply.

'Oh... No, I'm fine, thank you,' he replied, rousing himself out of his reverie. 'Sorry if I worried you. Just deep in thought. Trying to work some things out. Life's a bit confusing at times. But thanks for asking.'

'Well, as long as you're OK,' she said with a sympathetic smile. 'I just like to make sure our customers are OK. And we're not busy this afternoon, so take as much time as you like. But your tea must be getting cold. Let me bring you a fresh pot.'

There was a naivety about her that made her interest unthreatening. She was neither a practised professional whose job it was to care for others nor a zealous do-gooder trying to fix people. Just one human being expressing concern for another. And Ray found it moving, even healing. He wanted to say something that would adequately express his gratitude for her unfeigned humanity. What he actually said was, 'That's really kind of you. I'd love a fresh pot of tea.' He smiled at her as he said it. It felt like the first time he'd smiled at anyone for a long time.

# Twelve

## *Hospitality*

It was the Friday evening of Ollie's second week in Edinburgh since leaving Manchester after his mother's funeral, and he was due to set off the following morning for a gig in Aberdeen. It had been the oddest ten days or so of his entire life. A mind-boggling mixture of the good, the bad and the utterly confusing. Things with Ellen were definitely good. Far better than he had dared to hope. They'd met up for some time each day and spent most of their time together on long walks exploring the city and in even longer conversations getting to know each other. It was a new experience for him, but he assumed that this was what older people meant when they talked about 'courtship', a word that embarrassed him though he was never quite sure why. He was as physically attracted to her as he'd ever been to any girl. But, unlike his admittedly short-lived previous relationships, the objective of his attentions wasn't to get her into bed as quickly as possible. This was a longer game, a more demanding strategy with a far more serious goal. He wanted to get to know her, understand who she really was and how she'd become the person he found so fascinating. Since childhood he'd

147

always loved being the centre of attention. 'Ollie holding court again' was how his mother used to describe it. But now he found himself more eager to listen to Ellen than to talk about himself. She'd told him about her family, her childhood, and her teenage years. And he, in turn, had shared the story of his life to date, though he'd still said nothing about his father's infidelity and the extent of the gulf between them.

The bad part of those days was his continuing fierce anger, a simmering rage that had only been exacerbated by the news that had reached him from Tim Johnson of his dad's disappearance from home. It wasn't that he was concerned about his well-being, he told himself constantly. He didn't care what happened to him. He was just furious that the man who had regularly pontificated on the importance of responsibility to him in his teenage years now seemed to think that he could evade the consequences of his actions just by running off. And the utterly confusing thing was his guilt at his inability to grieve for his mother. He wanted to feel her loss deeply, to mourn her properly. But all he felt was a sense of numbness. It was as if the combination of his pleasure in his relationship with Ellen and his bitterness at his dad's disloyalty left no room for any other emotion.

He glanced at his watch and was surprised to discover that it was almost seven o'clock. He must have been lying on his bed turning all this over and over in his mind for the best part of two hours. It was time to shower and get ready for what promised to be an enjoyable evening. Charlie and Agnes had looked after him with an attentiveness that went beyond what he could reasonably have expected from the proprietors of a guest house, even sensitively checking that he was financially solvent and assuring him that if he was running short of cash, they were happy to regard him as a non-paying guest. 'You can just be a friend of the family,' was how Agnes had put it. There was nothing patronising about their kindness and they didn't fuss over him in a way that would have been irritating. They just seemed to like him and wanted him to feel at home. Normally, Ollie would have half-jokingly put it down to his good looks and charm, but there was something about the gentle and generous nature of their care that suggested that they felt a particular bond with the young stand-up comic who was staying in their guest house. And now they'd invited him to bring Ellen and join them for dinner with the promise that 'we'll make it a little bit special for your last evening'.

Agnes greeted Ellen warmly with a hug when she arrived just before half-past seven. Charlie looked on, clearly approving what he saw.

'Aah, you're the lassie he's been goin' on about since he got here. I can understand why. But already I'm thinkin' yer just too good for him.'

Ellen responded that she'd been thinking that herself, but that she'd taken pity on him and didn't want to send him packing just yet.

'Leave him alone, he's all right,' Agnes chipped in, her mothering instinct coming quickly to the fore. 'You men would all be useless without us. Ollie's no worse than the rest of you.'

Ollie was happy just to stand back and let this scene of happy domesticity play out before him. He'd told Ellen about his hosts and he was pleased to see that she was as comfortable in their presence as he was. He was even more pleased at how she looked standing in the hallway chatting easily with Charlie and Agnes. Previously he'd only seen her dressed casually in jeans. Tonight she was wearing a simple cap-sleeve knee-length white dress with a fitted waist. It had a bright ruby floral pattern that contrasted perfectly with her copper-coloured hair. He was certainly no expert on women's couture – though he did have a five-minute comedy riff on what he considered the ridiculous creations that were paraded on the cat-walks of the fashion houses – but he thought she looked perfect for a relaxed evening with friends.

Charlie and Agnes led them through into their immaculately tidy private apartment where the table had been perfectly laid with a Stewart tartan cloth for a candle-lit dinner. Four personalised gold-embossed cards marked each place and every piece of cutlery was set in exactly the right position. The Celtic sounds of Runrig were playing in the background to complete the Scottish ambience. Ellen couldn't contain her delight.

'Wow! This looks wonderful. You've gone to a lot of trouble.'

'Ach, we're happy to do it,' Charlie replied. 'We just wanted to gie Ollie – and yersel, of course – a taste of good Scottish hospitality before he sets off on his travels again.'

'Well, stop your blethering, Charlie,' Agnes interrupted. 'And get everybody sat so we can get on with this meal.'

Charlie dutifully did his wife's bidding and soon Agnes was bringing in the first course.

'It's Cullen Skink,' she said. 'And I hope everybody likes it.'

Ellen responded enthusiastically but Ollie confessed that he'd never heard of the dish, though he couldn't help remarking that there had to be some useful stand-up material in a name like that. Agnes explained that it was a soup made from smoked haddock, potatoes and onions.

'But I'll thank you not to be making jokes on some English stage about my good Scottish food,' she added, giving him a playful smack on the head.

Ollie promised to curb his comic instincts and they were just about to begin to eat when Charlie called for a pause in the proceedings.

'I'm no' what ye'd call a religious man. I leave that stuff to Agnes. But I always like to say grace at a meal like this and be thankful for what we've got. Ellen, ye'll be familiar wi' the Selkirk Grace, I don't doubt, so would ye' say it for us.'

She confirmed that she did indeed know the blessing to which Charlie had just referred and invited her fellow diners to bow their heads as she offered the prayer with which generations of Scots have preceded their meals.

Some hae meat that cannae eat,
An' some hae nane, but want it.
But we hae meat and we can eat,
Sae let the Lord be thank it.

Charlie responded with a loud 'Amen' immediately followed by an invitation to 'get stuck in', and after a few mouthfuls Ollie confessed himself to be an immediate convert to Cullen Skink.

The rest of the meal was equally successful. Agnes carried in the main course – Perthshire Venison Steak served with chicken liver pate, wild mushrooms, potato fondant and blackberry jus – to a chorus of oohs and aahs from her guests. And when that had been washed down by a dram of Charlie's precious single malt, to Ollie's delight she served up slices of Clootie Dumpling drenched in brandy cream. It was a dessert he hadn't enjoyed since he'd visited his grandparents as a child. In a flash he was on his feet, glass in hand, to propose a toast in his best Scottish accent.

'Raise your glasses, my friends. Here's to Agnes Stewart, the Queen of Cooks, to true Caledonian cuisine, and to the justly famed Clootie Dumpling. And may death and destruction fall on every Sassenach who perpetuates the vile slander that this is a nation that lives on deep-fried Mars Bars and Irn Bru!'

Agnes tried to look suitably modest at this compliment to her culinary skills, but the other two dinked their glasses and beat their palms on the table in support before all four of them dissolved in laughter.

It wasn't until the plates were cleared away and they moved to the lounge that the general hubbub began to subside. Over coffee and a generously laden cheeseboard with oatcakes and Agnes' home-made red onion chutney, the conversation gradually became more mellow and reflective. Ollie and Ellen sat together on the well-worn leather couch by the window, Agnes took the large armchair by the wood-burning stove and, to the amusement of his guests, Charlie grabbed hold of a cushion and settled himself on the floor leaning his back against his wife's knees.

'I've sat on the floor like this since I was a kid,' he explained. 'And I know ma place. Agnes treats me like her poodle anyhow. You wait. She'll tell me to get back into ma basket in a minute or two.'

His wife patted his head and their guests chuckled at the easy banter of the older couple and their obvious pleasure in each other's company. Ollie wondered what an artist might do with the scene and he momentarily visualised a sentimental Victorian study of two couples at very different stages of life. He felt a sharp pang of loss at the thought that he would never again sit with his parents like this. It was a passing emotion, but it must have revealed itself in his expression.

'Ollie, you're looking very pensive,' Agnes said. 'A penny for your thoughts.'

'Oh, I was just thinking… sitting here with you, enjoying your hospitality. It's really very special. I used to love seeing my folks sat together…'

Ellen moved closer to him and reached her hand out to his. Charlie and Agnes were wise enough not to respond too quickly, but to allow a stillness to linger long enough to give space for the conversation to move at its own pace. Agnes was about to respond, but before she could say anything Ollie picked up on his previous remark.

'And it's good to see a long-term relationship like yours, close and comfortable, but open and welcoming.'

Agnes smiled at him, but again nobody seemed in a hurry to react to his words. It felt to him like they were giving him permission to speak, waiting to hear what he'd say next. Encouraged by their quiet attention, he went on: 'Here's the thing I keep thinking about. I've turned up, without even having made a booking, and you've not only found a room for me in your guest house, but you've welcomed me into your home – like I was one of the family. It's beyond kindness. I can't get my head round it. I want to know what makes you the kind of people you are. '

As he was speaking Charlie got up from the floor, went into the kitchen, and returned with a fresh pot of coffee.

'Aye, right enough,' he said as he refilled their cups, 'we must be daft. But Agnes has aye had a soft spot for waifs and strays and I end up gi'en' into her. And we've looked after a few comedians of one kind or another in our time. Mind you, if I'd known ye were gonna bring a lassie round, I think I might have put ma foot down this time.'

He grinned at Ollie as he sat back down on the floor in front of his wife. Then his voice took on a more serious tone as he turned and spoke to his wife.

'G'on, Agnes. Ye'd better tell 'em our story. Otherwise they might start thinkin' that we're just two old fogies who like to interfere in other people's lives.'

Agnes nodded and put her cup down. She hesitated for a second or two as if she needed to prepare herself, like someone who was about to hop from one stepping stone to another in a flowing stream and who wanted to make sure they judged it just right to avoid stumbling and falling. The others noticed how still she had become and how carefully chosen and precisely articulated her words were.

'Charlie and I have been married for over forty years. We were like most young couples in our early years. We wanted some time together before we started a family. So we didn't start trying until after five or six years. For the first few years I didn't get pregnant and then there were several miscarriages. There wasn't IVF in those days, so we resigned ourselves to the fact that we weren't going to be able to have children. Then after eleven years it happened, and we had John. He was a great kid, full of mischief, easy to bring up, never got into any real trouble. He loved music and we got him a piano teacher. He had a real talent and we didn't have to make him do his practice. Came on in leaps and bounds.

'We were living in Inverness, we'd moved up there from Glasgow. Charlie ran his own business at that time, painting and decorating. Nothing big, but he's a good worker and always did a good job for people. So he was never short of work and we managed to save a bit. When he got to sixteen, John worked with his dad during the school holidays for a couple of years. I don't think he particularly enjoyed it, and he'd never have wanted to go into business with Charlie, but he appreciated the pocket money.'

She tapped Charlie on the shoulder and asked him to pass her a tissue from the box on the floor beside him. Ollie and Ellen sensed that this wasn't going to be a story with a happy ending and they expected her to wipe a tear from her eye. Instead, she folded the tissue neatly in half and placed it on the arm of the chair.

'That's just in case I need it,' she said smiling. 'I should really make Charlie tell you the rest of the story, but he's a big softy and he wouldn't be able to get to the end of it. So it's down to me. Now where was I? Oh yes... John got a place at the Royal Scottish Academy to do music when he was eighteen. We were very proud of him and we bought him a little car so it'd be easier for him travelling up and down to Glasgow. It was nothing fancy, just a second-hand Mini with a few miles on the clock. But he couldn't have been any happier if we'd bought him a Porsche. Charlie gave him all his driving lessons. They were just like a couple of kids with a new toy.

'Well, he was driving home on the A9 for the Christmas holidays at the end of his first term. Most of the road was still single carriageway back then. It was about six o'clock in the evening and a car coming towards him tried to overtake on a bend and hit John head-on. He died instantly.'

Ellen gave a little gasp and put her hand to her mouth. Ollie wanted to say something but couldn't summon the right words. Charlie put his arm over his wife's knees and pulled himself as close as he could to her. And Agnes just took a deep breath and went on with her story.

'Now this is not a pity party,' she said. 'But you've asked why we're the kind of folk we are and why we've welcomed you, Ollie. So let me finish my story. We were devastated, as you can imagine. It wasn't just the loss of our son, though that was bad enough. There was all the guilt about buying him the car. All the "what if" questions. For a little while we wondered if it might break our marriage. But we got through it slowly. I've always been involved in the Kirk. I had my faith and I got support from the folk there. They didn't try to give me answers – there weren't any. They just made sure they were there when I needed them most. It took Charlie longer than me. I think it's harder for a man. And Charlie's never been too comfortable with church. We just had to take it a step at a time.'

She stopped and took a sip from her coffee cup. Before she could speak again Ollie leaned forward, looking at her with a mixture of admiration and amazement.

'Agnes, I'd never have guessed from the way you two relate to each other and interact with your guests that you'd faced something like that. It's been hard enough for me losing my mum. But your *son* – how on earth do you ever get over that?'

She gave a little shake of her head and smiled wistfully.

'Oh, you don't get over it,' she said. 'We've never got over it. And we don't *want* to get over it. Getting over it would be like he'd never existed. And we never want to forget him. There's not a day goes by that we don't think about him or talk about him to each other. We lost our precious boy. It was terrible. We still miss him – every day. And nothing can bring him back. No... you don't get *over* it. But you do learn to get *on* with life. I can still remember the night – it must have been a couple of years after it happened – when Charlie and I sat talking about things, about what we were going to do. We knew we had to make a decision. We could just go on grieving. We could let ourselves get bitter about it all. Or we could be grateful for the time we had with John. And we could get on with life.'

For a moment she stopped and there was an expression of relief on her face, as if she knew she'd got past the most difficult part of her story.

'John was always inviting his mates round. You know what young lads are like. They're always hungry. And I'd cook for them. Often they'd stay for the night. We were forever making up the bed in the spare room or blowing up inflatable mattresses and fixing beds on the floor. The house was always like that when he was around, happy and noisy. He used to say to me, "Mum, you should run a bed and breakfast place. You're good at it." I'd always laughed. Never gave it a minute's serious thought. But it came to us that night. That's what we'd do. It would give us a fresh start. And it would give us the chance to do what we've always been good at – making people welcome. So that's what we did. We sold the business in Inverness, bought this place and this is what we've been doing for the last fifteen years. We never go back to John's grave. We think this is a far better way to remember him than moping around in a cemetery.'

Ellen, who had been sitting and listening intently, could no longer contain herself. She got up and rushed across to Agnes and threw her arms around her.

'Ollie's been going on about how kind you've been to him. I know he's really grateful. And I want to say thanks, not just for being kind to him and not just for this evening, but for what you've just told us.'

The two women held each other in an embrace until Charlie announced that he had something to add, something that Agnes hadn't mentioned. When he began to speak there was a tenderness in his voice, quite unlike his normal jocular tone.

'Agnes still hasnie fully answered yer question, Ollie. There's a wee bit more to it than she's told you. We noticed it first when ye stayed here a couple of years ago, an' even more this time. The thing is, *ye really remind us o' John*. I don't mean in some kin' o' spooky way. No' that at all. An'

158

it's no' so much that ye're like him in looks, though there is a resemblance. It's just that ye're so *like* him – the way ye walk into a room, the way ye become the centre of attention. An' we've loved havin' ye here. An' you, too, Ellen. If John had made it home that Christmas, he was gonna invite a girl to meet us that he'd met at college. And that didnae happen, of course. So you stayin' here, Ollie, an' you bein' here tonight, Ellen. That's been special for us. Somethin' we thought we'd never experience.'

Ollie sensed that it hadn't been easy for Charlie to speak as he had done, and he couldn't think of an adequate reply. So, instead of saying anything, he followed Ellen's example a few moments earlier, got to his feet and grabbed his host in a bear-hug. The older man responded warmly at first. But then he pushed Ollie firmly away and, with his hands on his shoulders, held him at arms' length. He looked him straight in the eye and spoke to him very directly.

'I need to say this to you, Ollie. I don't know what's happened between you and yer dad. An' it's none o' ma business. But I do know that life's far too short for family feuds. Ye've lost yer mam. Now don't lose yer dad an' all. Whatever it is an' whatever you have to do, put it right while ye can. Otherwise, ye'll regret it for the rest o' yer life.'

The atmosphere in the room suddenly became tense. Neither of the women dared to speak as the two men stood face to face. Agnes wondered if her husband had gone too far and Ellen was afraid that Ollie might react angrily to Charlie's plain speaking. The silence was heavy in the room until Ollie gave a low moan and swore quietly to himself. His legs seemed to buckle under him. Charlie

159

helped him back to his chair and sat him down. For most of the evening he'd been playing a supporting role to his wife. Now he took full charge of the situation. He asked Agnes to make some more coffee and then he gave his full attention to Ollie.

'Come on, son,' he said. 'I think you need to get some things off yer chest. Ye've been bottlin' it up since ye got here. Ye know ye're wi' friends. So ye can talk freely. An' ye can be sure it'll no' be talked about outside this room.'

At first Ollie's words came slowly, like water trickling through a tiny crack in a great dam. Then gradually, as the barrier of anger and resentment was breached, they began to flow until they tumbled out like a torrent carrying everything in its way. The disappointments of childhood, the injustices of teenage years, the bitter rage at his father's infidelity and hypocrisy, the throbbing pain of his mother's untimely death, all surged forth in a deluge of pent-up emotion. Wisely Charlie said little, only interjecting a phrase or a sentence here or there to clear a channel for Ollie's emotions to be released into. By the time the flood had run its course the clock in the hallway had struck midnight and the four people in the room were exhausted. But all four of them would remember that evening as long as they lived and none of them would ever regret it.

# Thirteen

## A Life in the Year

Just before ten o'clock on a late July morning, an unshaven middle-aged man dressed in well-worn jeans and a white T-shirt was opening the gate of a nondescript bungalow in a quiet side street in Chorlton. To a casual passer-by in that area of Manchester, his unkempt appearance and his weather-beaten face might have suggested that this was just another unfortunate soul who'd been living rough and who was hoping for a handout from the occupants of the house. But had they cared to take a second glance, they would have observed something in his bearing that told a different story. If his eyes betrayed a weariness, even a sense of resignation in the face of life's trials, then the firm set of his mouth and his unrelenting pace as he strode up the pathway sent out the message that this was a man who, despite everything, was refusing to give up. A man who had stood on the edge of a great and terrible abyss, but who was desperate to turn away from the chasm and determined to find a way back to a safer place.

He rang the doorbell and waited for a moment or two before ringing it a second time. When there was no immediate answer, he pulled his phone out of his pocket to check the address. A momentary look of impatience flashed across his face as he waited for a response. It had taken him an effort of the will to arrange this meeting and he wasn't at all sure that he could summon up the courage to make a second visit if there was no one at home. He visibly relaxed when he heard the sound of slow footsteps in the hallway.

The door was opened by a white-haired man in his late seventies. His grey flannels, argyle sweater and comfortable slippers reinforced the impression that this was not a man to be hurried into action by the sound of a doorbell. But he was obviously expecting his visitor and he greeted him warmly as he led him into the small front room.

'I'm Sam Andrews,' he said, stretching out his hand. 'And you must be Ray Young. I'm glad you've come. Tim Johnson told me that you'd asked to see me and I've been looking forward to meeting you. Let me make us some tea before we talk.'

The room was sparsely furnished with a couple of comfortable leather armchairs facing each other on either side of the fireplace and an old desk and chair in front of the window. While Ray sat himself in one of the armchairs, his host shuffled off to the kitchen and returned a few minutes later carrying a tray. His hands trembled and Ray, fearing that the teapot and biscuits might not survive the journey to their intended destination, quickly stood up, took the tray from his grasp, and set it firmly on the desk.

'Thanks,' he said without any embarrassment. 'Early stages of Parkinson's disease, as you might have guessed. A bit of a nuisance, but I usually get there in the end. Now, why don't you pour and prevent us both from getting scalded with hot tea?'

He smiled as he spoke, and there wasn't a hint of self-pity or annoyance at his condition in his voice. For the next ten minutes the two men made small talk over their tea and biscuits. It was the kind of conversation that normally serves no other purpose than putting both parties at their ease. On this occasion, however, Sam watched his guest closely and listened to his every word intently. Ray was aware that he was being scrutinised but he was neither uncomfortable nor annoyed by such keen interest. In truth, he was grateful to be the focus of someone's attention after such a long time travelling alone.

He was just beginning to wonder if the conversation would amount to nothing more than this when the older man seemed to take on a different persona. He was no longer just a benign elderly gentleman. Instead, as he put down his cup with a remarkably unshaky hand and sat forward in his armchair, he took on the air of a sage, a man who'd seen life and understood much.

'Now, Mr Young,' he said quietly, 'you need to talk and I need to listen. You don't mind if I call you Ray? Tim's told me about your wife's death and about what he called your "gap year". But I want to hear your story – as much as you want to tell me – from *you*. I'm not expecting anyone else today, so take your time…'

There was a breathy huskiness to his voice, the effects of his Parkinson's, no doubt. But as he spoke, Ray had the definite impression that the man sitting opposite, despite his physical weakness, had a strength of character that combined the deep wisdom of a philosopher and the stern authority of a prophet. He knew there would be no hiding the truth and that he'd need to tell his story honestly.

Sam's words hung in the air for a moment as Ray gathered his thoughts. Then slowly he began to explain his creeping crisis of faith and the sudden and tragic death of his wife in a very matter-of-fact and orderly manner. He spoke frankly and unemotionally about the affair with Annie Chaplin, the tensions with his son, his sudden flight from Manchester after the funeral, and his near-death experience in Bournemouth. It was as if he was talking about someone else, someone he knew and remembered only vaguely. He'd been speaking for ten minutes or so at that point and he paused, half-expecting a question or a comment from the other side of the room. But Sam Andrews just shook his head and said, 'Don't stop. I want to hear the whole story. What you've done and where you've been in the last twelve months – like I said, your "gap year".' Then he added with a half-smile, 'And you probably need to hear your story as much as I do.'

'Well, I certainly need to make some sense of it,' Ray responded. 'That's why I contacted Tim immediately I got back to Manchester last week and asked him if he knew anyone who might help me get some kind of handle on things. I've been on the move for the best part of a year. But it feels like a much longer journey than that. I know I can't stop where I am, and I'm not sure where I want to go or how to get there. I don't want to end up just going round in circles. Tim said you were the most reliable guide he knew. He warned me that you wouldn't let me waffle and you wouldn't just come back at me with some psycho-babble or glib pseudo-spiritual clichés.'

'Hmm... that sounds like Tim,' Sam laughed. 'He's a good man and an old student of mine, though he's maybe being a bit too complimentary to his old teacher. But get on with your story or we'll both end up just waffling.'

So for the next hour Ray gave an account of his travels after he checked himself out of the Royal Bournemouth Hospital. The kindness of the waitress he'd met in the tea room in Beaulieu had gone beyond bringing him a fresh pot of tea. As the café had emptied of other customers, she'd sat down and chatted to him. In the course of their conversation he'd told her simply that his wife had recently died and that he just needed to 'get away from everything' for a time. She'd asked where he was staying and her question had solicited the response that he had nothing booked and would need to find a suitable place to lodge. There was an easy solution to his problem, she suggested. Her folks lived in the house next door to a popular B&B. When it was full they would often help out by allowing their spare room to be used as ancillary accommodation. As it happened, the room was free that night if he'd like it. It sounded infinitely preferable to trawling around the New Forest villages trying to find a bed for the night and he gladly accepted the offer.

As things turned out, his one-night stopover stretched into a two-month stay. The parents of the young waitress were grateful for the extra regular income from their paying guest who was no trouble to have around their home and who spent the autumn days exploring the surrounding countryside or sitting quietly by himself in his room. And for Ray it proved to be something of an oasis, allowing him time and space to recover from his recent ordeals. He made weekly phone calls to Tim just to let him know that he was OK, but apart from that he contacted no one back in Manchester. On Tim's recommendation he registered with a local GP who was sympathetic and didn't press him for more details than he wanted to share. Ray told him only that he was 'a little depressed' and agreed to the suggestion that he should go on a course of antidepressants which helped to lift his mood and made it easier for him to cope with the uncertainty and anxiety of his situation.

His stay in Beaulieu came to an end when he returned to Manchester for the inquest into Jean's death in November. The hearing was mercifully brief and the Coroner's Court returned a verdict of accidental death. He took some comfort from the fact that there was no blame attached to the truck driver who was visibly upset and anxious to express his regret to Ray. The most likely explanation, the coroner concluded, was that Jean had driven into the back of the lorry having fallen asleep at the wheel. The knowledge that she would have been unaware of what was about to happen and would have died instantly at the moment of collision made it a little easier to bear. Ollie didn't attend the inquest, and that was both a disappointment and a relief to his father whose fears about how he and his son would relate to each other never materialised.

He remained in Manchester for just over a week, staying with Tim and his wife and returning to his own house only for a morning, just long enough to meet an estate agent and put the place on the market. There was just one thing more he had to do before leaving the city. On the last afternoon he met up with Annie Chaplin at the same coffee shop near the BBC studios where they'd gone on the morning of their first meeting. The last three months had been painful for her and she'd tried to contact him several times. Despite her tearful pleas, he'd never returned her calls. When he did get in touch with her to let her know he was in Manchester and to ask to see her, she'd wanted to meet at her flat. He knew better than to accept that invitation and had insisted on somewhere public. Their meeting was brief. He said nothing to her of his experience in Bournemouth, restricting his account of his travels to his stay in the New Forest. Now, he told her, he was going away for another six months or so in the hope that he would find some peace of mind and come to some clarity in his thinking about the future. She listened passively, only the occasional tear betraying the strain the encounter was placing on her. She asked just one question: 'So you mean it's all over between us?' And he could give her no answer other than that, though his feelings for her hadn't changed, he didn't know whether he would ever be able to resume their relationship. They both sat quietly for what seemed like an age, neither of them knowing what to say that would ease the pain of meeting and parting again so quickly.

As he got up to leave, Ray said, 'I'm sorry to cause you hurt. But I have to try to do what's right. God knows I've messed up enough already. I don't want to ruin your life too. Maybe it's best that you just move on, try to forget me, forget what's happened.' Before she could respond, he touched his hand gently on hers and then hurried to the door.

By five o'clock that evening he was back in his car and heading to the motorway. The compulsion to get away that he'd felt just after the funeral had returned with a vengeance, but this time he drove north to Scotland. His sister Mary, who'd never married and still lived in the Lanarkshire town where they'd grown up, was relieved to see him and more than happy to have him in her home after having heard nothing from him since the funeral. She took time off work to look after him while he tried to remember his younger self and the things that had shaped him. He visited the cemetery where his parents were buried, walked the streets of his hometown, and drove to some of the places he'd frequented as a child.

One morning he went looking for the old wooden 'holy hut', the scene of his youthful conversion, only to discover that it had been demolished almost ten years earlier and a tyre depot erected where it had stood. He wandered in, pretending to be a customer, but in reality trying to figure out where the old bench at which he'd knelt and prayed as a child would have been. As far as he could judge, the precise spot where he'd got to his knees and offered the 'sinner's prayer' four decades earlier was now occupied by a vending machine that dispensed soft drinks and sweets. He walked back out on to the street too depressed by what he'd seen to think about whether or not there was any significance or symbolism in the transformation of the place.

After a week he was ready to move on again. He'd wondered if a visit to his homeland would strike a chord in him, stir long-buried echoes of his childhood faith, or remind him of his roots and family. But the streets he remembered from childhood were changed as much as he was. He continued north as far as Inverness still hoping to awaken something within himself – nostalgia, hope, an aesthetic appreciation of the scenery, anything that would let him know that he was truly alive. Alas, his heart was colder and bleaker than even the Scottish winter and he turned south again with no idea where he wanted to end up. November had almost run its course and the trappings of the upcoming festive season were everywhere to be seen, which served only to darken his mood. For years Christmas had followed a firmly established pattern – an all-consuming and exhausting round of speaking engagements and events from which he would escape only after a late-night service on 24th December. Then it would be Christmas Day as a family. Ollie would usually head off again on Boxing Day, and that's when he and Jean would lock the door, refuse to answer the phone, and take a week to recharge their batteries for the coming twelve months. This year would be very different. He didn't even know where he was going stay for the next few days, never mind how he would spend Christmas.

Tim came to his help again in response to his telephone call as he drove down the M6, linking him up with an old friend of his who had entered an Anglican religious order in the south-east of England after university and who, at Tim's request, arranged for Ray to be a guest of his monastic community. He drove directly there, arriving late that night. It was agreed that he could stay for the next three months.

It proved to be a spiritual and emotional oasis. The daily round of prayer, stillness, and contemplation was very different from the evangelical tradition in which he'd spent his adult life with its dual emphasis on active ministry and intellectual assent to doctrines. It answered a deep need in him at that time. There was no pressure on him to sort out his confusion or address his lack of faith. He was allowed to be part of a community of believers who did not demand from him a certainty of belief that he had lost. As much as anything he came to appreciate the prayer that was offered corporately at Compline each evening. Its few well-chosen words, with their acceptance of human failings and hope for forgiveness, seemed to say more than many of the extempore prayers he'd struggled to compose for himself over the course of many years.

> Most merciful God, we confess to you, before the whole company of heaven and one another, that we have sinned in thought, word and deed and in what we have failed to do.
> Forgive us our sins, heal us by your Spirit and raise us to new life in Christ.
> Amen.[1]

It was to be the only prayer he could pray for many months.

As the days and weeks passed into months he began to recognise the need to prepare himself for the time when he would need to step back into the world again. As he allowed himself to relax into the quiet rhythm of monastic life and learned simply to *be* rather than to *do,* he was able,

---

[1] 'An Order for Night Prayer' in *Common Worship: Daily Prayer* (Church House Publishing, 2005), p.337. © The Archbishops' Council.

with the professional help of a local GP who was a lay member of the community, to steadily reduce his dependence on the antidepressants he'd been prescribed. There were still dark days, but they gradually became less frequent and a little less difficult than before. Nonetheless, he knew that he was far from ready to face the rigours of finding regular employment and setting up some kind of home. Fortunately, his house in Manchester had sold quickly and he had sufficient savings to allow him to take time before he needed to think about how he would earn his living.

It was Tim's old friend who acted as a kind of counsellor to him and who suggested in one of their conversations that he might consider going on a pilgrimage. It was a thought that had occurred to him more than once in recent years as he'd grown increasingly dissatisfied with his busy but hollow life. Now, the more he considered it, the more it seemed the obvious path to take. So, instead of leaving the community at the end of February as originally agreed, he stayed until the end of April. Early on the first morning in May he set off on foot from the bustling market town of St Jean Pied de Port in the foothills of the French Pyrenees to walk the Camino de Santiago.

He didn't expect nor did he experience any moments of life-changing epiphany along the 800-kilometre route. It was enough just to get up every morning and step out into whatever the day ahead would bring as he hiked alone or fell into step for an hour or so with a fellow pilgrim. Most nights he would sleep in one of the *albergues* dotted along the way. The dormitory accommodation was basic, but more than adequate for a man who was asking nothing more than to sleep well enough to cope with the next day. Occasionally, when his limbs felt particularly weary, he would break off for a few days and book himself into a slightly more upmarket *pensione* where he could rest and build up his strength for the journey. He had no responsibilities other than to rise each morning and follow the yellow arrows and scallop signs that marked the ancient pilgrim trail. No goal other than to walk the twenty or so miles that he'd set himself for that day. No need to seek any deeper meaning than facing the challenge to keep on the journey step by step, mile after mile.

After eight weeks on the road, he reached Santiago de Compostela on a hot and sticky July afternoon. He immediately made his way to the cathedral in time to join the congregation just as a nun was singing in a hauntingly clear androgynous voice. It was a sound that seemed to rise up from somewhere deep in her soul and made him shiver despite the sweat that ran down his face. As the echo of her voice faded away into the soaring vaults of the cathedral, eight red-robed men began to swing the *Botafumeiro*, causing the great bronze censer to pour out its incense smoke as it moved in ever greater oscillations high above the heads of the worshippers. It was a moment he would never forget but the meaning of which he could not fathom, other than that for him it signified the end of that part of his journey. He stepped out of the cathedral and back into the sunlight. There was a long queue of people waiting to have their pilgrim 'passports' stamped and to collect their *compostela*. No doubt, most of them would frame it and hang it on their wall as evidence of their piety and persistence – proof that their pilgrimage was over. Ray didn't join them. For him it felt more like a hiatus than a conclusion. A half-finished sentence rather than the end of a chapter. A cause for reflection rather than a reason for self-congratulation. It was time to go back to what had once been home, figure out if any of it meant anything, and see whether or not there was more to the story of his life.

# Fourteen

## Wise Counsel

Sam Andrews' attention had never wavered even for a moment while his guest was speaking. It occurred to Ray that such concentration must have been exhausting for a man in his condition and he tried to round off his tale quickly.

'Well, that's my story for what it's worth,' he said apologetically. 'I just hope I haven't tired you out too much.'

'Don't worry about that,' Sam replied. 'I can nap this afternoon. But a couple of things before you go. You're staying with Tim and Carol, that's right, isn't it?'

'Yes. They've been kind enough to put me up since I got back last week. But I can't impose on them for too long. I've got to work out where to go and what I should do with my life.'

'That was going to be my second question. Have you any thoughts on that... what you might do next now that you're back in the UK?'

Ray cupped his face in his hands and slowly exhaled before he answered the question.

'Not really. I know I can't go back to what I did before all this stuff happened. A man who's cheated on his wife, isn't in touch with his son, and has pretty well lost his faith isn't a man to be standing in a pulpit. The problem is...'

His voice trailed away as he searched for his words. Sam watched him closely and waited. The noise of a passing car on the road outside was the only sound that disturbed the stillness in the room. Ray later described it to Tim as 'one of Sam's intentional silences', a gentle but powerful emotional suction that drew the rest of the sentence out of him.

'The problem is,' he went on picking up where he'd left off, 'that I feel...' He struggled again to find the right phrase. 'I feel... *unworthy*. That's the closest I can get to it.'

Sam leaned forwards and fixed Ray with a piercing look. It was clear that he'd heard something he felt to be of more than passing significance. He raised his hand to indicate he wanted to pause at this point and he needed to alert Ray to the importance of what he'd just said.

'Hmm... that's an interesting choice of word,' he said thoughtfully. 'I half-expected you to say "ashamed" or "exhausted" – something like that. But "*unworthy*"? Why did you say that? What do you mean by it?'

The question momentarily unsettled Ray. Why had he used the word? It was only as he tried to explain it to Sam that he began to understand something that had been bubbling just beneath the surface of his conscious mind for months. His words came slowly as if he was dragging them up from somewhere deep and dark.

'Well, I could easily have drowned that night in Bournemouth. I *would've* drowned, probably *should've* drowned, if it wasn't for that young police officer turning up. I'm not even sure why I got into the water in the first place. I didn't even have the guts to make up my mind, do the job properly, just drown myself. And I didn't have the moral courage to turn and swim back to land. I just kind of let things happen. I could say that I'm *lucky* to be alive. But the thing is, I don't feel lucky. I just feel like a cheat. I couldn't make up my mind one way or the other. I couldn't kill myself and I couldn't turn back. I'm alive and I don't deserve it.'

He slumped back in his chair and looked across the room. The effort of dredging such an uncomfortable truth from his subconscious mind left him feeling weary and disconsolate.

'That's what I mean by *unworthy*.'

To his utter surprise Sam Andrews beamed at him for a second or two. His shoulders began to shake as he tried to restrain his laughter. Ray's first instinct was to feel annoyed at such an apparently flippant reaction to the costly personal revelation he had just made. Sam noticed his irritation and immediately stifled his laughter. He raised his hand again, a gesture that Ray came to recognise as his usual way of indicating that he had something to say that his visitor really needed to hear.

'I'm sorry, I don't mean to treat what you've said lightly. Quite the opposite, in fact. I'm just relieved and delighted to hear you say it.'

He was still smiling as he pronounced the word slowly, as if savouring its sound and meaning.

'Unworthy, eh? Unworthy... That's good. Very good. In fact, Ray, I think you've unlocked a door we all need to open for ourselves. I still remember when it opened for me. Do you know the story of St Ignatius, the mule and the Moor?'

Ray's irritation morphed into confusion, and he confessed that this was a tale with which he was unfamiliar.

'Well, it's a favourite of mine. And it always makes me laugh when I think of it. I first heard it years ago from an old Jesuit priest just after I'd been ordained as a Methodist minister, and it blew my narrow theology out of the water. Listen, the story goes like this...'

Sam paused for a moment and cleared his throat, as if preparing himself to recite a poem or declaim one of Shakespeare's great soliloquies, and Ray had the distinct impression that it was a story he'd memorised word for word, and one that he'd retold often.

'When he was thirty years old, Ignatius Loyola was travelling to the shrine of Monserrat on the back of a mule. Of course, he would later go on to found the Jesuit movement and would eventually be canonised, but at this time he still had the mindset of a soldier. At one point on the journey he was overtaken by a Moor – a Muslim, of course – and the two men rode together for a time. They fell into conversation about the Blessed Virgin to whom Ignatius was devoted. The Moor, however, was scornful of his belief that a virgin could give birth to a child. Ignatius became so angry and agitated at his fellow traveller's refusal to believe that the Moor took fright and hurried on ahead.

'After a time Ignatius began to question himself as to whether he had been sufficiently fervent in his defence of the faith. He grew so angry with the Moor that he was overwhelmed with the urge to catch up with him and stab him to death. But there was a doubt in his mind as to whether or not this was the right thing to do. Though he pondered deeply, he could not reach a decision. So he resolved on a plan. He dropped the reins and allowed the mule to ride on, unguided by its rider, until it reached a fork in the road. If it carried him along the path leading to the town where the Moor had gone, he would follow him there and kill him. If, however, the animal kept to the high road, bypassing the town, he would leave well alone and do nothing. The place where the road divided was no more than 100 yards or so from the little town where the sceptical Moor was seeking sanctuary. But the mule continued on the high road. The Moor's life was spared. And Ignatius was kept from committing murder – by a mule!'

Sam had told his tale soberly, even reverently. But now his face broke into a smile, and he started to chuckle to himself again.

'You're talking *unworthy*, Ray. Now what could be more unworthy than that? This is one of the great saints of Catholic spirituality, for goodness' sake! The Jesuits are still a force centuries later. Right across the entire spectrum of the Church his "spiritual exercises" remain the blueprint for people like me as we try to walk alongside other folk in their journey of faith and life. But the only thing that kept him from becoming a kind of one-man religious terrorist was a stupid donkey. It's just plain wrong to kill someone just because they don't believe what you believe. You know that. I know that. *He should've known that.* And it doesn't make a whit of difference whether you think the direction the mule took was the result of blind chance or whether you believe God was guiding the beast. Either way, Ignatius' inability to decide for himself was unworthy of any decent human being, never mind who he would become and what he would do.'

Ray was about to respond, but Sam hadn't finished what he wanted to say. He raised his voice and looked directly into Ray's eyes.

'We're *all* unworthy. One way or another we all get what we don't deserve. We get to be born because our parents copulated. We get to grow past childhood because they feed us and care for us. We get to stay alive because our heart keeps beating and our blood keeps pumping and our lungs keep inhaling and exhaling – even when we're asleep. We get to recover from illnesses because of the healing processes already in our bodies and the treatment we receive from the medical profession. We get to be good at doing some things because particular skills are wired into us. We get to be educated because generations who came before us reasoned things through and left us a body of knowledge.'

The smile had gone from Sam's face. He pounded his fist on the arm of his chair as he spoke.

'You know what, Ray? People like you and me – preachers and vicars and ministers, I mean – we've got a lot to answer for. We talk a great deal about grace and most of what we say is fine as far as it goes. But we've narrowed it down to a theological concept, shrunk it down to the point where it becomes a kind of shorthand for the truth that God forgives people who don't deserve it. So, the only people who've heard of it are the ones that sit in the pews every Sunday. And for most of them it only figures in their thinking when they've messed up and they need to ask for forgiveness. But it's so much bigger than that. It's the principle at the heart of the universe. *It's all about grace.* And we're all unworthy, unworthy of life itself – every breath we take is undeserved.'

Ray had anticipated meeting with someone who would fit his preconceived idea of a spiritual guide. Someone who would question him sensitively about his spiritual condition, listen and nod sympathetically, say little beyond asking him to clarify his statements, and tentatively suggest a course of action for his client to consider. Someone more like a professional therapeutic practitioner. But Sam Andrews clearly wasn't that kind of counsellor. And Ray's surprise at this passionate lecture on the nature of grace must have registered on his face, for Sam stopped and laughed again. Despite his uncertainty as to the nature of their encounter and where it was taking him, Ray couldn't stop himself from joining in the laughter. As Sam's laughter subsided, he spoke again.

'Listen, Ray, I graduated from the theological faculty of a good university with an intellectual understanding of grace. But a few years in pastoral ministry was long enough to teach me that grace seemed to make precious little difference to how most of my congregation thought about themselves and lived their lives. And when I first heard that ridiculous story of Ignatius and the mule, it acted like a kind of catalyst. I started to notice what had been staring me in the face – *that grace is everywhere* – to see that it underpins everything. And my perspective on life on this troubled but wonderful planet began to shift. Sure, there's a lot of human selfishness that needs to be forgiven and a lot of terrible suffering that still has to be healed. And sure, that depends on grace. But what constantly stops me in my tracks and fills me with enough joy to make me laugh like I just did, is how much grace is at work all the time, sustaining our very lives, keeping us from being our worst selves, saving us from pain, stopping us from following wrong paths we might have gone down. Sometimes it operates through other people doing grace-inspired actions and sometimes it appears to be just happenstance like Ignatius' mule. But it's there all the time. And if it wasn't, then we'd all be lost.'

His long tirade seemed to have left him exhausted, but Sam wasn't finished yet. He summoned the strength to get out of his chair and beckoned his visitor to do the same. Ray stood up, just a little embarrassed, wondering what was about to happen. Then Sam took hold of his right hand, and shook it with a firmness that belied his age and fragile health. There was a whimsical expression on his face that suggested a mock-seriousness in his action, but the timbre of his voice carried the authority of a monarch conferring a knighthood on a distinguished subject.

'Ray Young, welcome to the Alliance of the Unworthy. Whatever good you have done in your life and whatever guilt you carry, you are utterly dependent on grace. The purpose of your life is this: to live as a man who humbly and gladly accepts life as a gift, who accepts this grace and generously dispenses it to others.'

He let go of Ray's hand and lowered himself back into his chair.

'Now get out of here and get on with it. I'm tired so let yourself out, if you don't mind. And come back and see me next week at the same time.'

Sam had already closed his eyes and put his head back in his chair. Suddenly he looked like a weary old man. Ray felt that even to mutter a thank you would have disturbed his rest. So he slipped quietly from the room, out of the front door and back onto the street.

It was almost five o'clock before Ray returned to the Johnsons' house. Carol was in the kitchen and Tim was setting the table for dinner. He gave Ray a quizzical look.

'So, what did you make of Sam?' he asked. 'He's an unusual character. But I thought you'd find him helpful.'

'Unusual isn't even the word,' Ray laughed. 'Unique might be better. And he doesn't beat around the bush, does he!'

Before they could take their conversation any further, Carol announced that dinner was ready.

'Time to eat. Whatever you're talking about, you can finish it later. I know what you two are like. Let's get this while it's hot.'

The three of them contented themselves with the usual pleasantries over the meal, and it wasn't until Carol had gone off to meet a friend in the city, leaving them with instructions to clear the table and fill the dishwasher, that they resumed their conversation. It was Ray who began the exchange as they settled down with their coffee cups.

'Like you said, Sam's a character. It didn't go like I expected at all.'

'I'm intrigued,' Tim replied. 'But don't tell me any more than you want to.'

'That's OK. I probably need to talk about it. It'll help me get my head round it. On one level he didn't say anything I haven't known and taught for years. On another level, it was like I was hearing stuff, or at least *understanding* it, for the first time.'

'That's Sam,' Tim nodded. 'I've known him for more than thirty years and I can't fit him neatly into a category. Spiritual director, teacher, counsellor, prophet? Or just a wise man? But I'm all ears if you want to talk...'

For the second time that day Ray talked for an hour or more as he gave a report of his earlier meeting, and by the time he got to the end of his account, evening had given way to dusk.

'Sounds like Sam,' Tim said. 'And sounds like it definitely wasn't a waste of your time.'

'No, it wasn't. When I left his house it felt like a deep, persistent pain had begun to ease just a bit. You know what it feels like? Remember when I did my back in years ago? I went to the old osteopath somebody recommended, and he poked and prodded me for twenty minutes and then told me to get up and start walking properly. When I left his room the pain was easier and I was walking better than I'd done for weeks. And I said to you that I wasn't sure whether he'd actually *done* anything to my back or whether he'd just psyched me out of it. Well, *that's* what it feels like.'

They might have gone on talking, unaware of the lateness of the hour, had they not suddenly become aware of Carol standing in the doorway.

'What on earth are you two doing sat here in the dark?' she asked as she switched on the light. 'We have paid the electricity bill, Tim. And have you both gone deaf? Didn't either of you hear me let myself in?'

Ray felt just a pang of envy as the couple indulged in the kind of good-natured verbal jousting that often marks a solid marriage. For a moment the terrible 'if only' that had dominated his thinking for so long reasserted itself in his mind. This could all still have been his *if only*... But Tim had long ago learned how to read his friend's moods. And he was not about to allow whatever gains had been made that day to be lost. He quickly guided the conversation in a different direction.

'Ray, you must be exhausted after a morning talking with Sam and an evening going through it all again with me. Let's make a cup of tea before we all head off to bed.'

Twenty minutes later Ray was in his room and ten minutes after that he was asleep. That night he dreamed of receiving a gilt-edged invitation to a magnificent banquet. It was addressed to 'The Unworthy Mr Ray Young' and written in the most exquisitely crafted calligraphy. But when he woke up he couldn't remember how the dream ended and whether or not he'd accepted the invitation.

# Fifteen

## As Seen on TV

Two days had passed since Ray's encounter with Sam Andrews. Tim and Carol, sensing his need for solitude, made sure that they gave him space to be alone. His weeks of walking on the Camino in Spain had left him fitter and leaner than he'd been for some years and he'd gone for a run that afternoon, the first time since Jean's death. The exertion had tired him out, and after dinner he'd gone up to his room at half-past nine with the intention of getting an early night. He was just getting ready to go to bed when he heard Tim knocking on his bedroom door and calling out to him.

'Hope I haven't woken you up, mate. But there's something coming on TV that I think you might want to see.'

Ray was feeling more than a little irritable as he opened the bedroom door. His legs were heavy after his run and he couldn't think of anything that would be interesting enough to keep him sat in front of the television when he could be asleep.

Tim held out a newspaper with the page open at the TV schedules for the day. He'd circled the Channel Four programme for 10.30pm.

'Carol was checking the listings for a series she's been watching, when she noticed it. I wasn't sure what to do at first. But I thought I really should let you know.'

Ray took the paper and read the paragraph that Tim had highlighted.

ANYTHING FOR A LAUGH!
The second in a four-part series on the ups and downs of life on the comedy circuit. This week's focus is on Ollie Oldham, recently described by one critic as 'a preacher's son for whom laughter has replaced religion'.

'I managed to keep contact with Ollie for the first couple of months after the funeral,' Tim explained. 'But I haven't heard anything from him since then, so I'd no idea this was coming up.'

Ray was surprised to learn of the TV programme, but he agreed that he wanted to see it. He had very mixed feelings as he settled himself in front of the television, and Carol asked if he'd rather watch it alone. It was an offer he quickly declined.

'No, you and Tim better be ready to hold my hand,' he said only half-jokingly. 'Not sure how I'm going to react to this. I may be glad of some moral support.'

The programme was a hybrid – a combination of a comedy show, a documentary on life on the road, and a series of in-depth conversations filmed backstage after a performance exploring what kind of person would jettison the relative stability and security of a nine-to-five job for the uncertain life of a stand-up comic. Ollie spoke honestly about his difficulty in settling into either the dull routine of daily employment or the discipline of academic life at university, and then moved on enthusiastically to talk about the buzz he got when standing in front of a live audience. He recalled some of his earliest and most chastening experiences on the comedy circuit as he honed his skills in front of critical and unsympathetic audiences.

The three people watching the programme in a Manchester vicarage paid particularly close attention to an excerpt from one of Ollie's routines in a London comedy club where his tales of his upbringing and increasing disillusionment with church life – obviously exaggerated for comedic effect – brought a ready response from an audience who clearly shared his low opinion of organised religion. It was a topic that provided an easy segue to an obvious line of questioning for the one-on-one backstage conversation that followed.

'Isn't it odd,' the interviewer asked, 'for a preacher's kid to become a stand-up comic? I mean, it's hard to think of two more different professions.'

Ollie, however, insisted that they weren't as different as might at first be imagined. Despite his teenage rebellion and his adult rejection of his parents' faith, he was keen to stress that he'd learned a great deal from listening to his dad's preaching. In the age of the sound bite, he suggested, preachers and stand-up comics were really the only people who regularly get up in front of an audience and talk for any significant length of time. And both were trying to do something more difficult than simply impart information.

He paused to towel the sweat off his face and take a drink from a bottle of water lying on the table in front of him before continuing to draw a parallel between the comedy club and the pulpit.

'The important thing is,' he said sitting forward in his chair to emphasise the point, 'they both want to provoke a response. In my case, it's to make people laugh by showing them the incongruity of things, inviting them to embrace the absurdity of life. Preachers, I guess, are coming from a different angle, inviting people to see meaning in things, to have faith, to be forgiven or commit to a cause. But in both cases, to be effective, the guy upfront has to brew up a potent mixture of language and personality mixed with a particular point of view. It's a concoction that, when it's skilfully blended, will produce an alchemy that's difficult to explain but easy to recognise when it works.'

Just at that moment someone opened the dressing room door, gave the thumbs up and shouted, 'Great set, Ollie. You were really hot tonight.' He waved his hand to acknowledge the compliment, but he quickly returned to his topic.

'And another thing,' he went on, 'stand-up and preaching are unique forms of public communication. In both of them the same person combines the creative element and the performance element. I mean, comics and preachers write their own material and then they present it. You know, my old man didn't preach somebody else's sermons and I don't do somebody else's material. Good preachers and good stand-ups do all the work themselves. So it comes out of who they are and what they've experienced. And when they deliver it, the material comes through their personality. And, of course, in the presentation there's also an element of improvisation. My dad would tell you, I guess, that he responds to the promptings of the Spirit when he preaches. For me, I'm sensing the mood, watching the reaction of the audience and responding to that. If you're a preacher or a comic, who you are and what's happening to you inwardly matters as much as your prepared material.'

From the moment they had sat down together, Tim and Carol's attention had been as much on their guest as on the television screen. How would he react, they wondered, having not seen his son since the day of Jean's funeral? But Ray had sat very still, paying close attention without reacting in any way to what he was watching. Some shots of Ollie dealing with a couple of inebriated hecklers in his audience led into a commercial break and Carol took the opportunity to bring in some tea and biscuits as much to ease any possible tension as to provide some late-night refreshment.

'You OK, Ray?' Tim asked as he poured the tea. 'It must feel a bit odd for you, hearing Ollie talk about his upbringing.'

'It does, kind of. But I'm just relieved and grateful that there doesn't seem to be any bitterness in his words. That's what I was dreading most, if I'm honest.'

'Well, let's see what he has to say now,' Tim said as they turned their attention back to the television.

What Ollie had to say next turned out to be the most difficult part of the programme for Ray to hear. The interviewer's question that opened up the last segment of the programme was an obvious one, given the nature of the show.

'So was there ever any possibility that your life might have taken a different direction, that you might have followed in your father's footsteps and become a preacher?'

Ollie greeted the question with a rueful laugh, and slowly began to frame his answer.

'Naah... no chance of that. Like most other kids, when I was really young my dad was my hero. Even when I was too young to fully understand what he was talking about, I thought he was really clever to get up and address a congregation like he did every week. And I did think, I want to do that when I grow up. But by the time I got into my teens, things were pretty tense between us. It was partly just the normal teenage rebellion thing. But it was more that I just couldn't believe the stuff my parents believed. I didn't work it all out intellectually. It just seemed to belong to a different world and a distant time. I think I did try to believe it for a while. But in the end I couldn't see the point in it. It was just too much of an effort. And it got in the way of life itself.'

The follow-up question was another one that Ray could see coming and it was one he'd been dreading.

'So what does your preacher dad think about his stand-up comic son? Does he come to your gigs?'

Ray groaned audibly. He was conscious of the fact that Tim and Carol were trying hard to keep their eyes fixed on the television and not to look at him. Why, he asked himself, couldn't they just have made a bog-standard comedy show instead of including this probing questioning? None of the three made the slightest sound as they waited for the answer to come.

Ollie grimaced instinctively. It was obvious that he was less than comfortable with the direction the conversation was taking. But he'd agreed to appear knowing that it included the kind of questions that went much deeper than the typical celebrity chat show. His tone was quiet and his words were carefully considered.

'Hmm... he has been to a couple of my shows, but I don't think he's over the moon about what I do. And, of course, Oldham is a stage-name I've adopted and he's definitely not enamoured about that. But we haven't really been in touch since my mum died last year. It's not a great relationship, to be honest. Who knows, maybe it'll get better. We've both made our mistakes, I guess. It happens in families. But I don't really want to say any more than that...'

As his son's voice trailed away, Ray could hardly believe what he'd just heard. 'Maybe it'll get better...' Ollie had said. Could that mean there was some possibility that their relationship could be repaired? Was there some hope after all that had happened? It was more than he could have anticipated and something he'd never expected to hear on a television programme he didn't even realise was on air until an hour before. For the next few minutes he was vaguely aware of Tim and Carol laughing at one of Ollie's riffs on the perils of a routine visit to the doctor, but his mind was such a flurry of conflicting thoughts that he was oblivious to what was being shown on the screen. His attention was suddenly drawn back to the television by the brief exchange that preceded the concluding credits.

'So, what does the next year hold for you, Ollie?'

'Oh, more of the same, I hope. I'll be happy if I can go on doing what I love doing – making people laugh and getting paid for it.'

'And the rumours are that you're getting married? Doesn't fit your image at all. Is it really true?'

Ollie's face broke into an embarrassed grin.

'We thought we'd kept that a secret,' he laughed. 'But it's obviously out there. I met Ellen about a year ago and she's promised to make an honest man of me. We haven't sorted out a date yet, but it'll be some time before the end of the year. Some of my mates are surprised we're doing something so traditional. Maybe I'm just getting older and wiser…'

'Or maybe you're still more of a preacher's son than you realised? Maybe your upbringing has shaped you more than you thought?'

Ollie hesitated for just a moment.

'Maybe I am. And maybe it did…'

As the closing credits rolled, Carol touched her husband gently on his arm and slipped out of the room. Tim reached for the remote and turned off the television. He looked at Ray, who sat there shaking his head in disbelief, and wondered what his reaction might be to what they'd just heard. Neither of them was in any hurry to speak. It was Ray who eventually broke the silence.

'Wow! What should I make of all that. The preacher's son stuff. The "maybe it'll get better" line. And he's getting married! I wasn't ready for any of that. Where do I go from here? And what am I supposed to do with this?'

Tim knew better than to venture an answer to those questions. Instead, he laid his hand gently on Ray's shoulder and they sat together, allowing the silence to settle again on the room. Both men knew that enough had been said in the last hour. And both knew that the strength of their friendship meant more than their words ever could. It was well after midnight before they turned in for the night.

'I'm glad we were able to watch that with you,' Tim whispered as they parted company at the top of the stairs.

Ray nodded: 'Me, too, mate. Me, too.'

In their thirty years of knowing one another it was one of the shortest conversations they'd ever had. But it carried more significance than many of the protracted discussions that had been a feature of their long friendship.

For an hour or so after he went to bed, Ray replayed in his head the programme he'd just watched. The truth was that for the past year he'd pushed all thoughts of his son to the back of his mind. The seeming hopelessness of their broken relationship was more than he could cope with. And it had been as much as he could do to survive, to hold on to life from day to day. No point in torturing himself with an aspiration that could never be fulfilled. But now, with the image of his son on the TV screen sharp and clear in his mind, his longing for some kind of reconciliation and forgiveness flooded back into his consciousness. He began to form a sentence, unsure whether it constituted some kind of prayer or if it was simply an expression of a deep and desperate yearning. Despite his tiredness, his innate preacher's predisposition to distil big truths into memorable phrases reasserted itself. When he eventually dropped off to sleep there were seven words running through his mind like a mantra: *a just resolution and a genuine reconciliation*.

By the time he came down to breakfast the next morning, his hosts had already left home for the day. But a place had been set for him and lying just beside it there was a note in Tim's handwriting, neatly folded in half, with Ray's name in bold capital letters. He left it there until he'd made some toast and poured himself a cup of tea. His legs were stiff and weary after yesterday's run and he was in no mood to hurry. The thought of reading it made him just a little nervous. Last night's unexpected broadcast had raised a glimmer of hope and he was nervous, half-expecting that something would happen to extinguish it before it could even flicker into life. He unfolded the piece of paper slowly and read the message:

> Hope you slept OK. We're both out all day. Help yourself to whatever you need. There's a message on the answerphone from Sam Andrews. He's going to meet a friend tomorrow and thinks it might be good for you to meet her too. Can you call him and let him know? Have a good day. Tim

Ray picked up his phone a little reluctantly. His visit to Sam had been more helpful than he could have anticipated. But who was the friend Sam wanted him to meet? And why? He wasn't sure that he was ready to cope with meeting someone who'd made a heroic recovery from some moral mistake or tragic accident. That would just make him feel worse than ever in the light of his own predicament. But it would be ungracious and ungrateful not to return the call. So he decided to ask what this was all about and to be ready with an excuse if it made him feel uncomfortable. He took a deep breath and picked out the number from his contacts. No sooner had it begun to ring than he heard Sam's voice.

'Ray. Glad you called. I want to take you to meet Laura Sheldrick. She's an old friend of mine. Fascinating woman. I think it'll do you good to meet her.'

Ray hesitated for a moment, wondering how he could put this nicely.

'Sam, you were really helpful the other day. And I'm grateful to you for thinking of me. But I'm not sure I'm ready to meet somebody who's been brave and come back from a difficult time. It'd just make me feel worse at the moment.'

He could hear Sam chuckling at the other end of the phone.

'You don't need to worry. Laura's nothing like that. She's an artist. If I'm not mistaken, you'll love her stuff. It's no more than a half hour's drive to where she lives. And she always does a great afternoon tea. If you don't come away feeling better about things I'll leave you half of my worldly wealth when I die.'

Ray felt a flush of embarrassment come over him at his initial reticence and seeming ingratitude. It was impossible to refuse Sam's invitation when he put it in such terms.

'OK,' he said, responding to Sam's infectious laughter. 'Sorry for being so defensive. I'm a bit oversensitive, I guess. I'll be glad to come with you.'

'Great,' came the reply. 'Do you mind picking me up around one o'clock? I don't drive much these days and we'll be a lot safer with you behind the wheel. See you tomorrow afternoon.'

There was a click and Ray realised that the conversation was at an end. Sam didn't do small talk. He was beginning to understand how his new-found companion operated. His words were a means to an end and when the object had been achieved he was ready to move on. But Ray had a suspicion that Sam's purpose was more than just to solicit his appreciation of some *objets d'art*. What exactly that purpose was on this occasion, however, he couldn't immediately discern. But he had a hunch that meeting Laura Sheldrick would turn out to be as surprising and interesting as Sam himself had been on their first meeting.

# Sixteen

## The Beauty of Broken Things

It was a warm, late summer's day and the village of Lymm was looking its best in the afternoon sunshine when Ray drove into the car park and found the last empty space.

'So this is where Laura lives,' he said, switching off the ignition. 'Must be twenty years or so since I was last here. I'd forgotten how nice it is. She's chosen a great place to live.'

'We're not quite there yet,' Sam replied, struggling to ease himself out of the car. 'We've got a bit of a walk, but it'll be worth it. Do you mind giving me a hand? Just takes me a minute or two to get going again. I'll be fine once I've straightened up.'

Ray walked round the car and helped him onto his feet, and together, taking Sam's leisurely pace, they strolled through the village and over the bridge before turning immediately left and heading along the side of the canal. Its grimy, functional past, when its purpose was to transport coal from the Duke of Bridgewater's mines at Worsley to the industrial heart of Manchester, had long since faded into history. On a day like today it was a picture-postcard scene with freshly painted barges moored along the edges of the water and the kind of houses you'd expect to find in an upmarket estate agents' brochure spread alongside the towpaths on either side of the canal.

After ten minutes or so Sam paused, wiped the sweat from his brow, and pointed to a white two-storey cottage a couple of hundred yards further on at a bend in the canal. Unlike most of the houses on either side, which protected their privacy behind stone walls or wooden fences, this one fronted right onto the towpath. A narrow but lavishly planted and well-tended rockery was set against the white walls, giving it an air of welcoming cheerfulness. The impeccable appearance of the exterior suggested to Ray that the occupant of this residence was someone who combined good taste with attention to detail.

'That's Laura's place,' Sam said. 'Most appropriately named house on the canal, for my money.'

Ray wasn't sure why the house deserved such an accolade until he was near enough to read the green oval name plate with its embossed white lettering. It said simply, 'Laura's Place'. Before he'd even crossed the threshold he was forming a definite impression of the woman he was about to meet. She seemed to share Sam's penchant for coming straight to the point and he wondered what else they might have in common.

Before they could ring the bell, the door swung open and a woman of mixed race greeted them warmly. Laura Sheldrick was dressed in well-worn and slightly stained dungarees. There was, however, a natural elegance in her movements that her casual work-clothing could not obscure. Ray guessed that she must be in her early or mid-seventies, though she had that youthful sparkle that he'd often noticed in women who had a zest for life that the years had never managed to extinguish.

'Sam Andrews! It's good to see you,' she called out, throwing her arms round him and hugging him tightly for what seemed like a long time. 'It's too long since you've been to see me. What've you been up to, you old rogue?'

Ray stood back, uncertain as to whether she'd realised he was there and unsure what he should do. Then, as quickly as she'd embraced Sam, she released her hold and turned to greet the guest he'd brought with him.

'And you must be Ray Young. Sam's told me a little about you and I've been looking forward to meeting you. Says he's heard you like jazz, so you must be OK.'

There was a kind of easy confidence that exuded from Laura that at one and the same time made Ray feel immediately drawn to her and yet slightly awkward in her presence. It reminded him of schoolboy encounters with the smartest or best-looking kids in the class, when he'd been pleased to be in their company but also felt acutely aware of his own clumsiness or lack of sophistication in comparison to them.

Laura ushered them through the entrance porch and into a spacious lounge that had what estate agents like to call 'character features' in abundance. But the olde-worlde charm of the inglenook fireplace and exposed beams was in contrast to the eclectic mix of furnishings which had found their way from far-flung corners of the earth to this very English setting. A table from India, a Shaker rocking chair from America, a seventies-style Swedish sideboard, an old Mexican rustic wood-carved bench, a variety of antique Russian orthodox icons, Japanese figurines,

Chinese calligraphy, and paintings ranging from realistic portraits through impressionist landscapes to abstract cubism – all jostled cheerfully, and surprisingly harmoniously, for attention. But Ray's eyes were drawn past this colourful array to the unpainted exposed stone fireplace wall on which were hung dozens of photographs of a young woman in her twenties or thirties standing in front of a microphone, usually with a pianist, drummer and bass player behind her. Despite the passing of the years, she was immediately recognisable as the woman who had just welcomed them. Now he understood the import of her greeting when they'd stood on the doorstep. She'd been a jazz singer in her younger days!

'I told you you'd enjoy meeting Laura,' Sam said with the pleasure of a magician who's just amazed his audience by pulling a rabbit out of a top hat. 'I first got to know her when I was a student and she sang with her trio at our graduation ball. It was the first time I'd heard anybody sing like that other than on records. And she was good. She's too modest to tell you that she can still sing more than a bit.'

'And you're an old flatterer, Sam Andrews,' Laura laughed. 'And I'm forgetting what I should be doing. You both look hot. Let me get you something cool to drink.'

For the next half hour, sipping from a cool fruit punch, Ray listened with rapt attention as Laura, prompted regularly by Sam, recounted her experiences of singing with some of the best-known names on the London jazz scene of the sixties and seventies.

'They were great days,' she said wistfully. 'I'm still in touch with some of those guys, though a lot of them have passed on.'

'So why did you stop?' Ray asked. 'You must have had real talent to mix in the circles you did.'

'Well, yes,' she laughed, 'I did, I guess. But not quite the level of talent that would let me really break through to the big time. Then, of course, The Beatles came on the scene. That took popular music in a different direction and jazz was in the doldrums for a while. I'd been to art college before I started singing professionally and that was my first love. So it was time to do what I always wanted to do.'

'And that's what I really want you to see,' Sam chipped in. 'The jazz chat was just for starters. Laura's a sculptor and potter. You need to see the good stuff she makes.'

Laura obligingly led them through the kitchen and out to the back of the house where the garden was as meticulously set out as the rockery at the front. There was space for a lawn bordered with bright-coloured flowers, a neat shrubbery, and a well-tended vegetable garden. A gentle breeze rustled the leaves of the surrounding trees, the scent of summer flowers hung in the air, and the sound of birdsong could be heard all about them. It was an idyllic setting and it made Ray think of a word one of his university professors had been fond of using, a word he never thought he'd actually ever use himself. He smiled as he said it to himself. It seemed the perfect word to describe this plot of ground – *prelapsarian*. A place untouched by the imperfections of a fallen universe, a haven in which to cultivate a perfect garden and create objects of exquisite beauty untroubled and uncontaminated by the confusion of the broken world outside.

That impression was abruptly dispelled, however, when they entered the large garden shed which stood in front of a bank of trees at the bottom of the garden and served as Laura's studio. It took a moment for Ray's eyes to adjust to the relative gloom after the bright afternoon sunshine, but gradually he began to distinguish the outline of a potter's wheel on the bench by the far wall. On the shelf above there was a collection of pots of various shapes at different stages of completion, and in the right-hand corner of the room something he took at first to be a wood-fired stove, but which he quickly realised must be a kind of pyramid-shaped kiln. Everything had an unfinished and chaotic look which was in stark contrast to the order and harmony of the garden through which they had just walked. It wasn't until Laura pressed a switch in the wall, turning on a series of bright tabletop lamps, that he noticed over to his left several piles of broken pottery that he assumed had been discarded. He wondered why someone with an artist's flair for bringing order hadn't just put them straight in the bin.

His face must have betrayed his surprise at such untidiness for Laura immediately smiled at him and said knowingly, 'Ray, the creative process is always a messy business.' He was aware of Sam grunting approvingly in the background and he knew immediately that he was the victim of a conspiracy between the two of them. He was about to protest, but before he could think of what to say, Laura spoke again.

'I'm not entirely sure what Sam's up to, but he wanted me to show you what I'm spending most of my time doing these days. Have you heard of *kintsugi*?'

Ray had to ask her to repeat the last word. But hearing it for the second time simply confirmed for him that he'd never heard it before and had no idea what it meant, other than that it sounded vaguely Japanese.

'Well, you're right about that, at least,' Laura said. 'But I need to explain so you can understand about the broken pottery you've been looking at, and what I do. Let me tell you an old Japanese legend...'

The two men perched on stools while Laura began to tell her story. It was a tale, Ray thought, that must have been told over centuries in very different cultures and in very different places. But the timbre of Laura's voice and the cadence of her sentences, refined and schooled as they had been in the nuances of African-American music and the plaintive notes of the blues, gave it a unique life and a particular poignancy that day, especially to someone as sensitive to the rhythms of jazz as Ray. He listened intently as she told of a Sakai tea man in the sixteenth century who purchased a beautiful tea jar at great expense. So proud was he of his acquisition that he invited *Sen no Rikyū*, the renowned Japanese tea master, to join a gathering of his friends so that he could impress his visitor by serving him tea in the magnificent vessel. But to his great displeasure, his honoured guest showed no interest in the costly piece, but instead spent the time in deep conversation with the other guests and in rapt contemplation of a branch that was swaying gently in the breeze just outside the window. Such was his bitter disappointment that when his visitor had left, he threw the tea jar against a wall in a fit of pique, shattering it into pieces. His friends, being wiser than he was, gathered the fragments, took them home, and painstakingly put them together again. However, in their repair they made no attempt to hide the damage. Instead they joined the broken pieces, highlighting the cracks with a rich gold lacquer. Later they convened their own gathering to which they invited *Sen no Rikyū* and served him tea in the mended jar. The great master, who had been unmoved by the bowl in its pristine state, was deeply touched by its restored appearance and exclaimed, 'Now the piece is magnificent!'

A gust of wind tugged at the door of the shed. The creaking as it moved slowly on its hinges broke the spell that Laura's retelling of the ancient tale had cast. It had taken Ray not just to a distant land and different time but to a place deep in his being. He wanted to say something in response, but he could neither shape his thoughts nor form the words that would have articulated what he was feeling at that moment. Laura stood up and walked over to the shelf where the piles of broken pottery were lying.

'According to Japanese folklore,' she said, picking up one of the ceramic fragments, 'that was the origin of *kintsugi*. It means literally to "patch with gold". It's the very opposite to modern repair techniques which try to achieve a kind of invisible mending, to make the article look exactly as it did in its original condition. In *kintsugi* the point is to accept and even celebrate the damage as an integral part of the history and identity of the object. Instead of trying to hide the cracks, you highlight them by joining the broken fragments with gold lacquer. You make something with a different kind – I'd even say, at its best, a richer kind – of beauty to what it had before. Let me show you...'

She bent down and opened a cupboard under the shelf, carefully lifted out a bowl and held it up so that it caught the sunlight streaming through the window. The delicate duck-egg blue colour contrasted with the rich warmth of the gold veins that held it together. It was a union of seeming contradictions, an extreme fragility allied to a robust and regal strength.

They must have sat there for half an hour admiring and commenting on Laura's handiwork as she produced several pots and vases from the same cupboard. Ray had rarely seen anything more moving or more beautiful. Each one had been repaired by the same meticulous technique, each one with its own history and beauty, each one uniquely marred and each one uniquely restored. Such was their fascination with what they were seeing and handling, they might have stayed even longer had Laura not set the bowl she was holding gently down on the bench and announced that it was time for tea. They stepped out of the shed into the full light of the afternoon sunshine and took their places at a circular table on the edge of the lawn under the shade of a tree.

Afternoon tea turned out to be as pleasing as the setting in which it was served. Several different blends of tea were on offer and there were sandwiches in abundance with a variety of fillings on an assortment of different breads followed by a more than ample supply of scones, pastries, and cakes, all delicately prepared. The pleasure of the food was marred for Ray only by the thought of just how much

Jean would have enjoyed such a beautifully presented meal, and he had a crushing pang of regret and remorse as he recalled promising to take her for afternoon tea at Claridge's for their next wedding anniversary. The darkness that settled on him at that moment threatened to overwhelm the hope that had begun to stir in his spirit since meeting his host a couple of hours earlier.

He wasn't sure if Laura had noticed the change in his mood or whether she just decided that was the right time to share her story. Whatever it was that prompted her to speak, it was enough to pull him back from the brink of despair. As she filled their cups from a fresh pot of Earl Grey tea, she said that she wanted to share why she found the art of *kintsugi* so satisfying not only as an art form but also at a very deep level of her personality.

'I haven't told this to too many people,' she said. 'And I haven't even told the full story to you, Sam, though you're one of my dearest friends. But the older I get, the more important it becomes to me and the more grateful I am for it.'

Even back in the day when she'd been singing with those legendary jazz musicians whose photos adorned the walls of her cottage, Laura had never had a more attentive audience than the two men who sat in her garden that day. For a second or two their intense concentration on what she was saying almost unnerved her.

'Don't stare at me like that,' she laughed. 'You'll give me stage fright.'

Her unexpected hesitancy served only to increase the anticipation that Sam and Ray were already feeling, but they both tried to assume a laid-back pose which caused all three of them to laugh.

That was enough to dispel the tension. Laura made herself comfortable in her chair and began her story.

'I'm guessing you've noticed,' she said with a smile, 'that I'm mixed race. People weren't so politically correct about it in my childhood. I remember one of my teachers at primary school describing me as "that half-caste child". I wasn't exactly sure what it meant, but even as a kid I realised it wasn't intended as a compliment.'

Sam was about to interject with a sympathetic comment, but Laura stopped him with a shake of her head.

'No, that's not the point of my story. Quite the opposite, in fact. There are always people who will make unkind comments. But this is a story about amazing generosity. Listen...'

She paused momentarily. The sound of the breeze and the singing of the birds seemed to fade into the background and the garden felt very still as she picked up her tale again.

'See, my parents were both white. As you can guess, the day I was born, my mixed parentage was immediately obvious. It was a shock to everyone, especially my dad. It was only after giving birth that my mum confessed to a one-night stand with an American GI who'd been stationed near to where we were living after the war. Dad was away from home for a few days with his work, and she'd been to a party in a neighbour's house where they'd persuaded her to have a couple of drinks. She'd never had anything more than a glass of sherry before that and she was vulnerable to the charms of the good-looking African-

209

American in his uniform. Of course, this was before contraception was freely available and she'd been hoping against hope that she hadn't conceived on that night and the child she was carrying was my dad's. Those months during her pregnancy must have been agony for her. But the moment I arrived the truth was out – if you take my meaning...'

Laura gave a soft chuckle after that last sentence. As she began to speak again, the tone of her voice and the shake of her head suggested that even all these years later she still found it difficult to believe how things had turned out.

'My dad was magnificent. Sure, my mum's infidelity hurt him, but he forgave her. Told her he wasn't going to allow one wrong act destroy their relationship or obscure all the good things about her. And he was adamant that whatever the circumstances of the new baby's conception, this latest child was a blessing and just as much a part of the family as my two older brothers.

'The first few months must have been tough for them. You can imagine the reaction back in the 1940s. It set some tongues wagging. Dad refused to give any kind of apology or even an explanation, but of course people put two and two together very quickly. When the pastor of the little chapel they attended suggested that the christening of the baby should take place privately and not in a normal service to avoid offending or embarrassing other members of the congregation, Dad left, saying that if he'd forgiven Mum and accepted the baby as his own, then he wasn't going to allow anyone to treat his child as some kind of second-class member of God's family. And, when I was growing up, if anyone asked if I was adopted, he'd just say with a twinkle in his eye, "No, she just arrived looking like she does. Some kind of miracle, if you ask me." They never knew how to respond to that…'

Sam could contain himself no longer. 'Wow! What a man your dad must have been. Makes me wish I could have known him.'

'Sit down, Sam,' Laura laughed. 'I haven't got to the best bit yet.'

Sam sat back down a little sheepishly and Laura went on with her story.

'When I was in my teens and old enough to understand things a little bit better, Mum and Dad sat me down one day and told me the whole story. Said they were doing it for two reasons: they didn't want me to hear it from someone else and they never wanted me to think that they regarded me as an "accident" or an "unwanted child". I'll always remember Dad holding Mum's hand in his right hand and mine in his left and saying, "Your mum has apologised to me a thousand times. And she's regretted what happened that night at the party ever since. But you can't go back and undo things. What's done is done. And all that matters to both of us now is that good came out of it. We got you, and that's enough for me."'

Sam blew his nose hard and mumbled something about his hayfever being bad that day, which made the other two smile. Ray exhaled a long slow breath and admitted that what he'd just heard had given him a lump in his throat. But Laura hadn't finished. There was a postscript to her story, she said, that she needed to add.

'After Mum and Dad had both died, I decided to try to trace my natural father. I knew from what Mum had told me that his first name was Tony and I had some snippets of information about his military service and his time in England. It wasn't easy, but in the end I traced him to New York, only to discover that he'd died six months earlier. That was a disappointment, that I never got to meet him. But I did go over and visit his family, who were very kind. I spent a week with them and they told me all about him. What affected me most was when they told me he was a jazz musician, a saxophone player. Just an amateur, never did it professionally, but he was by all accounts a decent player. I'd often wondered where I got my love of jazz from. Mum and Dad weren't musical at all. So all of that came from him. I am who I am because of my mum's mistake, her moment of weakness, what the pastor of the little chapel called her "terrible, terrible sin" when he refused to christen me in a regular Sunday service.'

Laura stood up and began to clear the table. Sam and Ray followed her example, gathered up the cups and saucers on to a tray, and followed their host into the kitchen. There was a lot to think about and nobody spoke while they loaded the dishwasher. Then all three of them stood for two or three minutes looking out of the window onto the garden. Eventually Laura spoke very softly.

'When I was introduced to *kintsugi* it seemed like the perfect kind of art form for me. I love my life, I've had so much happiness, and I'm grateful for every moment. And I often think about the fact that it's all been the result of broken pieces, the failings and weaknesses of human beings.'

She put her arms on the shoulders of the two men who were standing on either side of her.

'You know what?' she said. 'I think my old dad was the ultimate *kintsugi* artist.'

There wasn't much either Ray or Sam could add to that, other than to express their thanks for a wonderful afternoon and take their leave. But as they drove home, Ray recalled his initial reaction to the garden and the almost-forgotten word that had sprung to mind: *prelapsarian*. Now, however, he thought to himself that it was utterly inadequate after all they had heard and seen that afternoon. Now there was an old Latin tag forcing its way into his mind: *felix culpa* – the happy fall. And he could even remember the words of St Augustine he'd mugged up on for an exam when he was a student: *Melius enim iudicavit de malis benefacere, quam mala nulla esse permittere.* Sam had dropped off to sleep after the exertions of the day, so he allowed himself to repeat the words and their English translation quietly to himself. *For God judged it better to bring good out of evil than not to permit any evil to exist.* If only he could be sure that was true…

# Seventeen

## A Shared Allegiance

It was just after seven o'clock on a Thursday evening in the vicarage of St Thomas' Church. Tim Johnson had gone off to a meeting, his wife, Carol, was downstairs tidying up after dinner, and their guest was lying stretched out on his bed gazing up at the ceiling. A couple of weeks had passed since Ray had gone with Sam Andrews to visit Laura Sheldrick, weeks in which he'd gone over the impressions of that afternoon in his mind again and again. Was the beauty of Laura's *kintsugi* art really a parable for life? Could damaged lives and broken relationships be restored in a way that gave them new meaning and purpose, despite the irreparable consequences of past wrongs and the permanent scars left by deep hurts? Or was all that nothing more than a pious notion that would quickly be crushed by the hard knocks of life in the real world? And these were questions of more than merely philosophical interest for Ray. He knew he couldn't stay with Tim and Carol for too much longer, and the time was rapidly approaching when he'd need to make some decisions about his future. The only certainties in his mind were that he'd messed things up, that he could never turn back the clock, and that life could never go back to what it had been before. But where could he go from here? And would his life ever have any worthwhile purpose again? To all these questions he had no answers.

He might have lain there turning all this over in his mind until it was time to switch off the light and retire for the night had his melancholy thoughts not been disturbed by the ringing of the doorbell. He took little notice at first, assuming that the visitor must be either a parishioner with a pastoral need or a friend of Carol's coming to spend the evening with her. He was vaguely aware of the sound of women's voices coming from downstairs and someone being shown into the room that his hosts used to receive callers. Then there was the creak of the stairs and a tapping on his bedroom door.

'Ray,' Carol called quietly, 'are you awake?'

He got himself up quickly and opened the door.

'There's a woman downstairs. Says it's really important she speaks with you. She seemed reluctant to say more than that, but I'm pretty sure she's genuine. We get some odd callers here, but she's not like that. She's a strikingly attractive young woman.'

'Well, I've no idea why she'd want to speak to me,' Ray countered. 'But I'll take your word for it. Just give me a minute and I'll be right down.'

As he walked into the small downstairs reception room, the young woman stood up to greet him. Though he did not know it then, he was not the first member of his family to be struck by her sparkling green eyes and shoulder-length copper-coloured hair.

'Mr Young,' she said stretching out her hand, 'I'm really glad to meet you. I'm Ellen Kilpatrick, Ollie's fiancée. I hope you'll forgive me calling unexpectedly like this.'

He was taken aback and needed some time to gather his thoughts. So this was the girl his son was intending to marry. But why had she come to see him? On her own? And how should he respond to her greeting? He managed to pull himself together and shake her hand.

'Well… it's nice to meet you, too,' he stammered. 'A bit of a shock, if I'm honest. But sit down and tell me why you've come.'

Sitting across the room from the man who would soon be her father-in-law and who was estranged from her future husband, Ellen's natural confidence suddenly deserted her. She could feel her heart beating faster and she gave a nervous cough to clear her throat. She made a deliberate effort to sound calm as she spoke.

'Mr Young, Ollie's told me about the problems between you and him, and about the death of your wife. He really misses his mum and, if he's honest, he's missing you too. Deep down he knows he needs to start to put things right with you. He's not short of confidence in front of an audience, but he's not nearly so self-assured when it comes to talking face to face about really important stuff. So I'm wondering if I can help you two get together – if you'd be willing.'

Ray couldn't help but admire the young woman sitting opposite him. It must have taken a great deal of courage to come and talk like this, not knowing what kind of reception awaited her. He also felt an unexpected surge of pride in his son. Whatever disagreements they might have had over the years, Ollie had clearly made a good choice of a wife. He desperately wanted to respond positively to her offer. But the bitter memory of his meeting with Ollie in Edinburgh and their parting at Jean's funeral caused him to phrase his reply carefully.

'Well, before I answer that, I need to ask you a question. Does Ollie know you're here?'

Ellen shook her head.

'No, he doesn't,' she admitted, before adding with a knowing smile, 'but you can leave Ollie to me. You can trust me to deal with your son. I just need to know that you're willing before I work on Ollie.'

That was the moment that broke through Ray's defences. It brought countless conversations he'd had with Jean when Ollie was going through his rebellious teenage years flooding back into his mind. Whenever father and son had reached an impasse in their frequent confrontations, she'd always known how to deal with the boy, always been able to step in and bring some level of compromise or resolution. Now he was talking to another woman who'd taken over that role and was bringing some hope of the reconciliation he'd longed for. He'd only met her five minutes earlier, but he was willing to pin all his hopes on her. His voice wavered a little as he spoke.

'Of course I'm willing to do what it takes. I want it more than anything else in my life. Tell me what you have in mind. And please call me Ray, by the way. Mr Young makes me feel old.'

Ellen visibly relaxed when she heard Ray's answer. It was clear that that was what she'd been hoping for. She leaned forward and spoke in confidential tones with the air of a conspirator who knows that her latest scheme can only succeed if she has a willing accomplice.

'We're staying at a hotel here in Manchester for the weekend. Ollie's got a gig at the Dog and Bone Comedy Club tomorrow evening and we don't need to set off again until Sunday afternoon. He's told me about how you two clashed when he was a teenager. But he also talks a lot about the times when you were often happiest together. And I think I know the best place for you to meet...'

For the next ten minutes Ellen outlined her plan. Ray listened carefully and asked questions until they were both satisfied that they'd come up with something that if not 100 per cent foolproof, at least had a reasonable chance of success. Their strategy was all but complete when they heard a tap on the door and Carol's voice.

'I don't want to interrupt, but I thought you might need some refreshments,' she said as she set a tray of tea and biscuits down on the coffee table.

Ray quickly introduced Ellen, explaining that she was Ollie's fiancée. Carol nodded and shook hands with their guest.

'Call it woman's intuition, if you like, but I had a feeling that's who you might be. I couldn't think why else an attractive young lady with a Scottish accent would be calling on us and asking for Ray on a Thursday evening. And it seems to me you two haven't wasted any time on small talk.'

'No, we haven't,' said Ray. 'We've had what I hope will turn out to be a very productive conversation.'

'And I'm guessing that you've probably got more you still need to catch up on, so let me leave you to continue your conversation.'

They talked for another hour after Carol had left the room. Ellen was keen to learn about Ollie's life in the years before she'd got to know him. And she in turn told Ray about how they'd met and how their relationship had developed from that first encounter.

'And sharing a cup of tea with you,' she explained as she concluded her update of their life together thus far, 'is more significant than you might realise. Ollie first saw me when he was doing a lunchtime gig in a pub. He told me that I stood out for two reasons. He spotted my red hair, of course. But he also noticed that I was the only person there drinking tea. I've been a tea addict all my life – since I was a child. When other kids were drinking fizzy drinks and that kind of stuff, I was drinking tea.'

To anyone else that might have seemed an insignificant personal detail, but to Ray it was just another cause for hope.

'I hope he's picking up your liking for tea. I've been worried about his drinking for a while.'

Ellen's assurance that she'd definitely seen a change in that aspect of Ollie's life simply served to endear her to him even more. This young woman seemed to have an influence for good on his son that gave him a glimmer of hope for the future. As he stood at the front door watching her drive away, he hardly dared to think about what he'd just agreed to. But maybe more could be mended than he'd ever expected.

When Ray woke on Saturday morning, his first flush of optimism at Ellen's proposal had all but evaporated, to be replaced by a sense of foreboding. What had he been thinking of two nights before when he'd agreed to what now seemed like a harebrained scheme with the undeniable potential to make things worse than ever? He even toyed with the thought of breaking his promise and just not turning up. But the problems that might throw up for the future seemed, if anything, an even less attractive prospect.

He parked his car shortly before two o'clock, feeling like a man about to face major surgery in which the odds were stacked heavily against survival. Turning left and joining the growing crowd walking up Chester Road, his mood lifted a little as his individual identity was absorbed into something larger. This was the tribe to which he and Ollie had belonged for so many years, a company of men and women whose personal problems could be forgotten for a couple of hours on a Saturday afternoon while they concentrated all their attention and emotional energy on a shared allegiance against a common enemy. But whether or not that shared passion between him and his son would be enough to bridge the hostility that had separated them for so long was something about which he had no certainty.

For some reason that he couldn't understand, it suddenly occurred to him that the distance from his car to the spot where he'd promised to meet Ellen was almost exactly the same as that between the two piers in Bournemouth. That was a walk he'd taken more than a year ago, not knowing what he was going to do or how it would end, and he reflected again that he'd survived that night through no merit of his own. The walk he was taking now was not all that dissimilar. He had the same sense of being caught up in something beyond his control, and that thought was enough to plunge him into a black melancholy that was in sharp contrast to the exuberance and excitement of the people around him.

For a moment he considered just turning around and heading back to his car. He had little hope of being so fortunate a second time. By then, however, he'd drawn level with the Bishop Burns pub where the songs and chants of the drinkers who spilled out onto the pavement reminded him of the ten-year-old who would stand next to him singing loudly and trying to remember his dad's instructions to miss out the obscenities that too frequently formed part of the lyrics. Whether it was that memory or simply the volume of people heading for the same destination that prevented him from turning back, he couldn't be sure. Whatever the reason, he went with the flow until it turned into Sir Matt Busby Way, where the crowds streaming in from the tributary roads formed an irresistible tide. There was no hope of going back now. Within two or three minutes he was standing under the statue of the man from whom the thoroughfare took its name and right in front of Old Trafford Stadium. He glanced upwards as he had done so often on a Saturday afternoon to see the enormous red lettering that proudly announced MANCHESTER UNITED.

Ellen's logic had seemed impeccable when she'd outlined her plan. She knew that deep down Ollie wanted to begin to put things right with his dad. And she knew from all he'd told her that some of his happiest memories of growing up centred on those times when they'd gone together to watch United play. It was, she had suggested, the ideal place to meet. The owner of the Dog and Bone where Ollie had been performing normally went to every home game with his wife and son. Much to his disgust, however, a relative had decided to get married on that Saturday. So, as part of his deal with Ollie, he'd given him his tickets and the three of them could sit together, surrounded by another 75,000 people, focus on the game, and 'just see how things went from there'. They wouldn't have to plunge straight into deep conversation or start addressing all the problems of the past. That could come later. This was just the initial encounter to re-establish the relationship. On Thursday evening, delivered in Ellen's lilting Highland accent, it had sounded like it might just work. Alas, it didn't sound nearly so convincing to Ray at twenty minutes to three on a Saturday, standing there scanning the crowd, half-hoping that Ollie had bottled it.

For the third time that afternoon he was on the verge of walking away when he felt a touch on his arm and turned to see Ollie and Ellen standing in front of him. For a few seconds the three of them formed a little island of quietness in the middle of a sea of noise and bustle, father and son looking at one other, neither knowing what to say and both fearing to speak, each dreading the other's reaction. It was Ray who took the risk and spoke first.

'It's good to see you, son. I've missed you. And I'm so sorry – for everything.'

Ollie took a step forward and threw his arms round his dad.

'Me, too,' he said. 'Me, too.'

To the people hurrying past to get to the turnstiles and take their places, it would have appeared an unremarkable scene. 'Under the statue of Busby' was an oft-repeated phrase when Mancunians arranged to meet up at the stadium before a match. It had been the setting for thousands of handshakes, back-slaps and manly hugs over the years. But seldom, if ever, was there a more significant reunion than the one that had just taken place. Neither Ray nor Ollie could think what to do or say next, so Ellen took command of the situation.

'Come on,' she said, getting between them and taking each of them by the arm. 'There'll be plenty of time for you two to talk. But I haven't been to a professional football match before, never mind to Old Trafford.'

They went through the turnstile and climbed the steep stone stairs to the middle tier of the North Stand without either man knowing how to restart their brief initial conversation. Nothing was said until they emerged from the grey concrete concession area into the light of the stadium. Ollie couldn't contain his delight when they discovered that their seats were positioned above the halfway line, the perfect viewing point for a football match.

'Oh, yes!' he exclaimed. 'This is alright. Way better than where we used to sit together behind the goals in the family stand when I was a kid.'

That was enough to release a torrent of reminiscences about those distant days when, in Ollie's memory at least, United had never lost or even played badly. Ellen, who was sitting between them with a knowing look on her face as they talked across her like excited schoolboys, imagined that this was what it must have been like in the days when father and son would have walked to the stadium hand in hand. So far, so good, she thought to herself. The time for deep conversation and the healing of old wounds would come later. For now it was enough that they were together enjoying their shared passion for the beautiful game.

It was only when the line-ups for both teams were announced over the stadium tannoy that Ray realised the importance of this match. He'd been so out of touch with things and so worried about meeting his son that he hadn't given any thought as to who their opponents would be that day. The sight of the Arsenal players coming on alongside the United team and the sound of the raucous chants of their supporters corralled in the far corner of the ground provoked the home supporters to raise the volume level by several decibels. This was not just another match. This was one of the games of the season, one they would have anticipated for weeks in years gone by.

When the referee blew his whistle for the kick-off, Ellen found herself sitting between two men who seemed to have totally forgotten her existence, something she didn't mind one little bit. About twenty minutes into the game, Ray leaned across to Ollie and offered his opinion that it really needed a goal to liven things up. His words seemed to have the power of an incantation when just seconds later they were celebrating the opening goal for United. And that proved to be just the start of one of the most magical afternoons they'd ever spent watching football together. By the end of ninety minutes the score was an incredible *Manchester United 8 – Arsenal 2*. Neither of them could recall an afternoon to equal this one. And Ellen could hardly believe that events had conspired to provide the perfect backdrop against which the drama she had planned had been played out.

When 75,000 people stood to their feet to applaud the victory at the final whistle, the man on Ray's right, with whom he'd exchanged approving comments and high-fives after a couple of the goals, shook his head in disbelief before turning to him and saying, 'My granny was right. There really is a God! I've just become a believer.' To the speaker, it was nothing more than a light-hearted comment, but to Ray it was heavy with irony. If only... he thought to himself as the crowd spilled out of the stadium; if only it was that simple. But he'd been to far too many football matches over too many years to allow himself to be deluded into thinking that some higher power was directing things to work out as well as they had done on this afternoon. Football was a game of luck as much as skill, and the bounce of the ball was down to mere chance rather than to the intervention of a divine being answering the prayers of one set of fans against those of another. They could play against exactly the same team next week and end up with a completely different result. And that wasn't any different to the rest of life, he reflected as his brain slipped back into the moralising mode of the *Pause for Thought* segments he'd presented on the radio for so many years. But never had he delivered any of these with the bitter cynicism that overtook his thinking at that moment. 'Yes, friends,' he imagined himself saying, 'life is just like that. Sometimes you win, sometimes you lose, and neither has any meaning or proves anything at all.'

No sooner had those negative thoughts asserted themselves than the sound of Ellen's voice broke into his self-absorption. Despite the mass of people pressing in on them from all sides, she was still managing to walk between them with her arms linked into theirs.

'Ray, I thought you'd be singing after a victory like that, but you haven't said a word since we left the stadium. Penny for your thoughts.'

'Sorry,' he replied. 'I *was* lost in my thoughts. But they wouldn't be worth even a penny. And you're right, we should be celebrating. And not just the score. It's been a great afternoon – thanks to you.'

Ollie registered his agreement with those sentiments and the three of them took their cue from the people around them and chatted happily about the game they'd just witnessed. And just as quickly as the dark thoughts had lodged themselves in Ray's mind, they were swept away by feelings of immense gratitude. He was alive, he had good friends who loved him, he was in the company of his son whom he had thought he might never see again, and his team had won! Of course, there were no easy answers to life's big questions, there was no way of rewriting the past, and there would always be doubts and regrets. But a football match had more than one lesson for life. What he'd always appreciated most about an afternoon in the stand watching his team play was that it absorbed his attention totally, causing him to live in the moment, accepting triumph and disaster as part of the cost and integral to the very nature of the thing that gave him such pleasure. Now *that*, he reflected without a hint of cynicism, would make a decent topic if he ever did *Pause for Thought* again.

# *Eighteen*

# *Bridge Over Troubled Waters*

A week after his meeting with Ollie and Ellen at Old Trafford, Ray was boarding a plane at Manchester Airport in the company of Sam Andrews for the one-hour flight to Belfast. They settled themselves into their seats and listened while the cabin crew went through the obligatory safety presentation prior to take-off. Sam was unimpressed by what he was hearing.

'Hmph…' he grumbled to himself. 'I could get that talk down to one sentence. If this plane comes down over the sea, shut your eyes, pray hard, and you'll quickly discover what you really believe in.'

Ray chuckled in agreement, but his travelling companion's wry comment set him thinking that just a few years ago he wouldn't have needed an imminent catastrophe in mid-air to remind him of the things he believed in. At the drop of a hat, he could have recited the ancient creeds, quoted from the writings of the Church fathers, made reference to the works of a dozen major theologians, and articulated his personal commitment to the central tenets of the Christian religion in a vocabulary that was jargon-free and, he hoped, reasonably accessible to his contemporaries who didn't share his faith. And it wasn't as though he had consciously rejected any of that. He certainly hadn't embraced a militant atheism or even slipped unthinkingly into a passive agnosticism. It was just that it all seemed so formulaic, so archaic, so out of sync with the realities of everyday life.

What had once been a vibrant and dynamic set of convictions now reminded him of wandering through some overgrown and neglected burial ground trying to read the words on the gravestones. Originally they would have carried an unambiguous message and given a seemingly permanent witness to lives that had been well-lived in conformity to beliefs that were firmly established beyond doubt or question. Sadly, however, the passage of the years and the ravages of time had eroded the letters and made them increasingly difficult to decipher to the point where they had become no more than worn and indistinguishable markings on cold stone. Now he wondered what would actually happen if Sam's ironic observation turned out to be an accurate prediction of disaster. What would he be thinking and to whom would he be praying if the plane suddenly nosedived into the cold waters of the Irish Sea?

The sudden rush of power as the pilot released the brakes and applied full throttle pinned him back in his seat and jolted him out of the perplexed mood that Sam's half-jocular comment had brought on. He'd never had a problem with air travel. As someone who had a fear of heights and who hated standing near the edge of any structure that was more than a few feet off the ground, it had always surprised him that he actually enjoyed flying.

The moment of take-off had always produced in him a sense of exhilaration. He could still remember the excitement of his first experience of air travel when he'd flown out of Glasgow on a typically miserable grey day, and his sheer delight when the plane had soared through the clouds into a clear blue sky bathed in a brilliant sunshine the like of which he'd never expected or even imagined before. Others might clutch the arm of their seat in terror or close their eyes in an attempt to overcome the oppressive feelings of claustrophobia induced by the confines of an aircraft. But getting airborne always lifted Ray's spirits, and today was no exception. They were not about to drop from the sky, he was not about to be ushered into the unknown, and there was no immediate pressure to do an audit of his beliefs. He began to relax.

When the steep climb of take-off levelled out and the morning sunshine began to penetrate the cabin, his thoughts, too, became brighter. He looked back on a week that had been happier than any he'd spent in recent times. It had started, of course, on the Saturday with the biggest margin of victory and the highest scoring game he'd ever witnessed. He'd often rebuked himself that his moods were influenced by the success or failure of his team far more than should have been the case for a mature adult. Despite that, there was no denying that those ninety minutes at Old Trafford had got his week off to a great start.

On the Sunday morning Tim had been unusually persistent in persuading him to come to church with him. He'd gone mainly out of loyalty to Tim, only to discover when they got home that Tim had had an ulterior motive for getting him out of the house, and that Carol had invited Ollie and Ellen to lunch. It had felt a little awkward at first, but Carol had known what she was doing having the five of them sit round the table together. She and Tim gently steered the conversation, avoiding topics that might have exposed deep hurts that would need much longer to heal, and Ellen entertained them with the story of her early encounters with Ollie and how their relationship had grown from there. She even managed to persuade Ollie to tell them of their growing friendship with Charlie and Agnes, of the fact that he was lodging with them more or less permanently when he wasn't on the road, and of the influence for good that the older couple had been on both of them.

Inevitably, that had led to the subject of their wedding at the end of the year. Again it was Ellen who took the initiative in breaking the embarrassed silence that stalled the conversation for a few tense moments.

'Look, there's no point in beating round the bush,' she said, holding Ollie's hand and stretching across the table to touch Ray's arm. 'I know you two are going to need time to sort things out between you. But Ollie knows that I've no intention of marrying him without his dad' – she paused and smiled at Tim and Carol – 'or his dad's best friends being there. So we'd better all get that straight right now.'

Having delivered her ultimatum, she emphasised her words with an exaggerated nod of her head that caused her copper-coloured hair to fall over her face and made her, and everyone else around the table, laugh. It was a gesture, completely unplanned and wholly natural, that made any response other than total acquiescence utterly futile, and allowed the conversation to flow easily into comfortable small talk and reminiscence.

When Ollie and Ellen had left to set off on their journey north, the others stayed round the table for another hour or so, drinking coffee and reflecting gratefully on what had just happened. Even Carol hadn't expected the meal to go quite as well as it had, and all three of them sensed that a start had been made that weekend on forging a path to reconciliation between father and son. Ray was careful to acknowledge that there was still considerable debris, mostly of his making, to be cleared away before he and Ollie would be able to walk that road together. But for all that, he shared his friends' gratitude for the progress that had been made. And as he helped Carol clear the table and fill the dishwasher after Tim had gone off to lead Evensong, he realised that for the first time in a very long time he was actually thinking of life as a long and winding road. It was, he knew all too well, a road into the unknown, a journey into a future where little could be predicted and where nothing was certain. But that was infinitely preferable to the dark impenetrable wall which had surrounded him for so long, stifling him emotionally and blocking any possibility of progress.

Over the next couple of days Ray had begun to think seriously, without coming to any definite conclusions, about what he might do with his life. He could reasonably expect to have another twenty or thirty years ahead of him. How would he spend them? What could he find to do that was meaningful and fulfilling? How could he build a future when what had been the two great bulwarks of his life – his faith and his marriage – were no longer there? And what about Annie Chaplin? She'd begun to come back into his thoughts in recent weeks and he knew that the attraction he had felt for her was as strong as ever. At the very least he owed her some kind of explanation or apology. But he had more than a suspicion of what it would mean if he made contact with her and that thought was enough to stir up anew his feelings of guilt at how he'd treated Jean.

It was time to talk to Sam Andrews again, set out the options, and get his advice. So he'd called on Sam on Thursday morning, tumbled out his thoughts and girded himself for an onslaught of blunt speaking. Sam's response wasn't what he had anticipated.

'Yes, it's about time you started thinking about your future. Can you be free this weekend?'

'Well… yes, I guess I can.'

'Then I'll try to book us a flight to Belfast. I'll take you to one of my favourite places. My grandad used to take me there when I went on holiday with my folks as a kid. It'll be worth the visit, I promise you.'

That was as much as he could get out of Sam that day. The old man didn't seem in the mood for extended conversation and wasn't about to offer any further counsel. Ray might have been offended at his brusque manner had he not, even in the relatively short time he'd known him, come to understand that, as Tim had put it to him, 'Sam was Sam.' You had to take him as you found him at any given moment. You never doubted that he was a good man. But there was also something just a little dangerous and untamed in him. Ray could think of a number of men he respected, but very few in whose presence he'd felt something that came close to what he might describe as a sense of awe. Sam was certainly one of that exclusive company.

That's why he found himself on a flight to Belfast on a bright, clear Saturday morning, not knowing exactly what his companion had in mind or where he was going to take him. Even when they disembarked on touchdown Sam still offered no explanation other than saying that they needed to pick up the rental car he'd booked in advance. It wasn't until Ray had turned on the ignition and asked where they were heading that Sam offered a clue as to their destination, though he still wasn't giving much away.

'Just head for the Causeway Coastal Route,' he said. 'It's the most glorious stretch of road anywhere. We'll stop at a place I know for a bite to eat before we head on a little further.'

Ray had been to Northern Ireland a couple of times to speak at conferences, but he'd always flown straight home and had never seen anything of the country. As soon as they turned onto the coastal road it was clear that Sam's opinion of its glories was fully justified. They drove northwards through a rich and varied tapestry of changing colours and contrasting landscapes. The bright blue waters of Belfast Lough, the deep verdant greens of the Antrim Glens, the long golden stretches of unspoilt beaches, the dark promontories casting their shadows on the sea, the stark whites of the cottages and lighthouses scattered along the route – all combined to make it one of the most impressive drives Ray had ever taken. Sam, despite his high praise, seemed largely uninterested in their surroundings. He was happy enough to let Ray take it all in while he caught up on his sleep. When the braking of the car woke him from time to time, it was obvious that his mind was on the destination to which they were heading rather than the picturesque countryside they were passing through.

They stopped in the small seaside town of Ballycastle at a takeaway fish and chip shop that Sam had known since childhood. Ray's initial disappointment at having to eat lunch sat on a wall was quickly supplanted by his enjoyment of fish and chips which were as good as any he'd ever had and which, Sam insisted, tasted all the better for being eaten out of doors, with a plastic fork, out of a polystyrene plate, with a sea-breeze blowing on your face. They finished off their meal with piping hot tea drunk from polystyrene cups which, as Sam again pointed out, perfectly matched the plates.

It was obvious from his manner that having slept for much of the journey, he was now feeling well-fed and wide awake. They drove the short distance to the tiny fishing village of Ballintoy where they parked the car and started down a steeply gravelled path for just over half a mile. With every step they took, the noise of the razorbills and guillemots that colonised this coastline became louder and more cacophonous. Sea-birds in the afternoon, however, had a very different effect on Ray from the rooks at dusk that had haunted his worst nightmares since childhood. He was aware of something undeniably wild and dangerous in the sight and sound of these creatures existing on the edge of the land and finding their food by diving into the cold waters of the Irish Sea. But there was also something life-affirming, a hint of what it might mean to live beyond the narrow limits of the security with which we surround ourselves, a sense of freedom against which our desire for comfort and safety block our path.

Ray suddenly realised that while he'd been lost in his thoughts, Sam, who was walking at an unusually brisk pace, was twenty feet ahead of him. He hurried to catch up and wondered to himself if this was really the same elderly man, suffering from the symptoms of Parkinson's disease, that he'd helped out of the car and who'd walked so slowly and with such effort through the village of Lymm just a couple of weeks earlier. Sam was obviously now in high spirits and relishing the prospect of what lay ahead. There was something in his manner that made Ray feel nervous at what this man who'd become his mentor and counsellor might have in store for him, and it wouldn't take long for him to realise that his uneasiness was well-founded. He'd noticed a sign saying something about a bridge as they'd got out of the car, but he wasn't prepared for the sight that came into view. His worst fears became a hideous reality as he looked with horror on the rope bridge slung 100 feet above the crashing waves below and spanning the sixty-feet chasm between the mainland and a tiny island.

'Welcome to the Carrick-A-Rede Rope Bridge,' Sam said. He paused in anticipation of Ray's response.

'You old so-and-so, Sam Andrews. How you got to know, I've no idea. But you've obviously found out that I don't like heights.'

'I seem to remember that Tim mentioned it once in passing, and I stored it up. Thought it might prove to be useful getting you to start living again. But at least I'm going to pay for us to cross over to the island. So that should make it a little easier for a Scotsman like yourself.'

Ray could feel the panic begin to rise as he stepped gingerly onto the bridge behind Sam. He clenched his fingers tightly round the ropes on either side and tried to close his eyes and ears to the sight and sound of the water surging below. Logic told him that the National Trust would never allow paying customers to set foot on the structure unless it was safe. But, as it swayed in the breeze and bounced with every footstep that he took, logic was not in control of either his mind or his body. His thoughts were racing, his mouth was dry and his heart was pounding as he trusted his weight to the slender wooden slats beneath his feet. Sam was walking steadily and deliberately ahead of him, seeming to have no fear at all. Unusually for that time on a Saturday there was no one else crossing just at that moment which, to Ray's horror, allowed Sam to pause, turn towards him and give him a short résumé of the history of the bridge.

'The original bridge was probably constructed by salmon fishermen around 300 or so years ago,' he said with the aplomb of a professor addressing his students in a lecture theatre. 'When I was a kid it had only one handrail and there were big gaps between the slats. It was really scary back then. But they've renewed it several times since 2000, most recently in 2008. It's really very safe these days.'

Then, as he began walking again, he called out over his shoulder, 'You're doing OK, by the way.'

They made it to the far side of the bridge and Ray threw himself down on the grass, closed his eyes and allowed his breathing to slow down to something approaching normal.

He wasn't sure how he'd managed to complete the crossing, other than that he'd successfully fought off an overwhelming desire to kill Sam, and just as unsuccessfully attempted to stifle a string of expletives that would have shocked any sensitive soul within hearing distance. When he'd recovered sufficiently to put a sentence together he asked Sam, 'What on earth are you playing at, bringing me here and making me cross that hideous thing?'

Sam was in no hurry to respond. With some difficulty he slowly eased himself into a sitting position on a nearby rock and said nothing for several seconds. His reluctance to speak made Ray feel that he was being challenged to find the answer to his own question.

When Sam did begin to speak, his whole demeanour had changed. Until a few moments ago there had been a roguish air about him. Now he was serious, like a man who was about to reveal a deep and precious secret that he shared rarely, and then only with those who had earned the right to know.

'This has been a special place to me – a kind of holy place, if you like – ever since I was a kid. I must have been about ten or eleven years old when my grandad brought me here for the first time, and when I tried to cross the bridge, that was the first time I knew what it meant to be really scared. Of course, he was crossing with me, watching me carefully, making sure I was OK. But it was still scary for a kid. And even more terrifying when I had to get back on to it again to cross back to the mainland.'

'Sounds to me,' Ray interrupted, 'that he was a cruel old so-and-so making a kid cross that thing. Come to think of it, that's probably where you got your mean streak from.'

Sam shook his head and went on.

'No, I loved the old boy. He wasn't cruel or mean. But he paid me the ultimate compliment you can pay to a child. He never talked down to me. Always treated me like an equal, albeit one who still had lots to learn about life. And I think he saw his role not so much as *teaching* me, but more as helping me to *learn life's lessons for myself*. Which is why he brought me here and got me to cross the bridge with him.'

'Still seems to me a bit of an extreme way of helping a kid get over his fear,' Ray objected again.

'No, it wasn't really about that. He had a bigger aim in mind than just toughening me up. Every time we came over to Ulster on holiday my sister would go off somewhere with my folks and my grandmother for the day and he and I would come here. It became a family tradition – 'Sam and Gramp's day', we used to call it. Each time we'd cross the bridge, sit down just near to where we are now, get lunch out of his backpack and talk. I can still hear his Belfast brogue all these years later.'

There was a brief pause while Sam got his handkerchief out to wipe his eyes and blow his nose loudly. This time Ray resisted the temptation to interject a comment and waited for him to continue.

'The last time we did it was the summer before I was about to leave home for university. I was the first generation of my family to get to university and, with all the arrogance of an eighteen-year-old who thought he knew what life was all about, I'd declared to my parents that I'd outgrown faith and that I was now an atheist. Grandad was the pastor of a little independent church in the Shankill Road and my folks were worried about how he might react when they told him of my teenage apostasy. But he never argued with me, didn't even make any reference to it, and he and I had our day out together, same as always. That's when I learned why we came to the Carrick-A-Rede Rope Bridge every year. And it's why I've brought you here today.'

Sam stopped speaking and tried without success to push himself up from the rock he was sitting on. Ray quickly got up and helped him to his feet. His first reaction was to wonder why an elderly man who must be wearied by the day's exertions would want to stand up just before he got to the point of his story. One look at the resolute expression on Sam's face, however, immediately reminded him of their first meeting when his host had dragged himself out of his armchair and stood to welcome him to the 'Alliance of the Unworthy'. It was the same action and the same determination that the import of his words should not be lost. They stood face to face. This, Ray thought to himself, must be what it would feel like to be in the presence of an ambassador bearing solemn tidings on behalf of a head of state.

'We were just about to pack up and go home when my grandad asked me to tell him about my loss of faith. He listened without saying a word while I must have talked for a quarter of an hour or so. I thought he'd argue with what I'd said or preach me one of his old fiery sermons. But all he did was to put his arm on my shoulder and tell me to remember four things from our visits to Carrick-A-Rede:

> the bridge may look slender, even precarious, but it's been here a long time and it's stronger than it looks;
> when you're scared to walk across, always ask yourself whether the problem is with the bridge or with you;
> and don't ever forget that, in a dangerous place like this, it's safer and wiser to trust the bridge than to risk your life in the waters crashing against the rocks.

That was the last advice he ever gave me. And that was the last of our excursions together. He died at the end of that year. I've never forgotten his words. And I've come back here most years since then on my own. In fact, this is the first time I've ever brought anyone with me. So consider yourself privileged indeed.'

Before Ray could think of the right response to make, Sam turned and set off back to the bridge.

'Come on,' he said. 'It's time to head back down to Belfast. My sister's going to put us up for the night.'

The stomach-turning realisation that he needed to cross the bridge again came over Ray like a wave of nausea. It was only the prospect of spending the night on this dark and cold outcrop, rather than any kind of native courage, that gave him sufficient nerve to trust himself to the fragile, swaying construction that would haunt his nightmares for weeks to come. He trudged after Sam and stepped onto the narrow wooden slats for what he hoped would be the last time in his life. When they reached the other side and stepped on to the mainland again, his head cleared enough for him to notice that Sam had not completed his account of his grandad's advice.

'You said there were four things he told you to remember,' he queried. 'But you only gave me three of them.'

'Oh, yes, the fourth one,' Sam said, stroking his chin and feigning an absent-minded expression. 'The fourth one... let me think. Oh, yes, now I remember: *if you get yourself stuck on an island, the hardest thing of all is to get back on the bridge again and walk back to the mainland.*'

They walked to the car together and the only sounds were the crunch of their feet on the gravelled path and the cries of the guillemots overhead. Enough had been said that day and neither of them felt the need for any further conversation.

# Nineteen
## Tales of the Unexpected

It was a cold and damp mid-November morning in Edinburgh. The weather was that characteristically disagreeable mix of fog and drizzle that is common in that part of the world and is perfectly described as a 'scotch mist'. A middle-aged man with a grey herringbone 'newsboy' cap pulled down over his eyes and his coat collar turned up against the wintry chill was hurrying along the Royal Mile on his way to a meeting, the prospect of which filled him with considerable trepidation. When he drew level with Prince Charlie's Tipple he pushed open the door and stepped inside. He'd been there only once before but, as his eyes scanned the room with its dark-wood floors and furnishings illuminated by the yellow light from the suspended lamps, the memory of his previous unhappy visit came flooding back. There was a lurking fear at the back of his mind that this encounter might end in a similar way. Not for the first time in recent months, he wondered if he'd done the right thing in agreeing to the meeting. His arrival probably hadn't been noticed and he could still turn around and head back into the street

Before he could translate that fleeting thought into action, he heard a familiar voice calling out to him.

'Dad, I'm over here.'

Ray Young looked in the direction from which the voice had come and made out the figure of his son Ollie sitting at a table in the corner. There could be no turning back now. He took off his cap, stuffed it into his pocket, turned down his collar, and walked across the room.

'Good to see you, son,' he said, a little nervously.

'And you, too, Dad,' Ollie responded. 'Really good to see you.'

If any of the other patrons that morning had overheard them address one another, it would have seemed an unremarkable preamble to a conversation between a father and his son. For the two men in question, however, the moment was charged with a sharp poignancy. It didn't escape the notice of either of them that those were exactly the same words with which they'd started their previous ill-fated meeting in this place, a realisation that imbued them both with the determination to make this a more fruitful encounter.

Ray took off his coat and sat down, still feeling awkward despite Ollie's warm greeting. He'd driven up from Manchester early that morning in response to an email from his son the evening before asking if they could get together for breakfast and specifically requesting that they should meet at Prince Charlie's Tipple. It seemed a long way to travel just for breakfast, especially at such short notice, and the choice of venue struck him as odd in the light of what had happened the last time they met here. But Ollie's email had sounded urgent and something told him that he needed to accept the invitation without question. Sam Andrews' words as they left Carrick-A-Rede had replayed themselves in his mind for weeks: *if you get yourself stuck on an island, the hardest thing of all is to get back on the bridge again and walk back to the mainland.* He knew he was stuck and he knew it was time to get back to the mainland of life. His difficulty wasn't just his fear of the precarious nature of the crossing. The real problem was that he still felt hemmed in by a thick mist of guilt and loss. He couldn't even locate the bridge, never mind start to cross it. How a visit to Ollie might help to lift the haze he'd no idea. But, when you're lost, you have to head in one direction or another and hope it gets you to where you want to go. Apart from all that, he reckoned that he'd a lot to make up to his son for after all the events of the last year and a half. He did wonder if something had gone wrong with Ollie's relationship with Ellen. Or maybe he was in some financial difficulty, something that wasn't unknown in the years since he'd left home. Whatever the reason behind the request, he clung to the hope that the progress they'd made a couple of months earlier on their visit to Old Trafford and their Sunday lunch together with Tim and Carol wouldn't turn out to be a false dawn before the fog rolled in again.

He was just about to say something to get the conversation going when Ollie gestured to the young man who was standing by the bar. As he approached the table, Ray realised with a sinking feeling that it was the waiter who'd served them the last time they'd eaten breakfast here and who'd witnessed their quarrel at close quarters. He braced himself to deal with what he expected to be an embarrassing moment, but he was totally unprepared for what happened next.

'Jamie, you remember my dad?' Ollie said when the waiter reached the table.

'Yes, I do,' he replied as he shook hands. 'It's Ray Young, isn't it? Good to meet you again.'

Ray returned the greeting, trying to sound as natural as he could, but he was at a loss to know what else to say. Ollie sensed his discomfort and took command of the situation.

'Dad, I guess you must be wondering why on earth I've asked you to drive all this way to meet me here. I'll explain everything in a minute. But first Jamie needs our order. I'm guessing that it'll be the full Scottish breakfast for both of us?'

Ray agreed and noticed Ollie and the waiter grinning at each other. Something was going on, and, whatever it was, they were both clearly in on it.

'It'll be the full Scottish for both of us,' Ollie confirmed. 'And this time we'll both behave ourselves and I promise not to cuss and scare your customers. Oh… and I'll be paying!'

While they waited for their meal to arrive, Ollie began to relate his story. It had all begun, he explained, a few months after their noisy altercation. He'd stayed away from Prince Charlie's Tipple hoping that anyone who'd witnessed the incident would forget it over time. But one evening he'd happened to run into Jamie in another Edinburgh watering hole and they'd fallen into conversation. After they'd talked for some time, Jamie had ventured to ask how things were between him and his dad, and that had led to Ollie launching into a bitter tirade about Ray being nothing more than a hypocrite. Jamie had listened quietly until Ollie had exhausted his store of pent-up anger, before tentatively suggesting that maybe things weren't that simple, maybe life wasn't as straightforward as that, and maybe he needed to cut his dad some slack. It wasn't something he was ready to hear at that time but, despite his initial irritation at what he considered to be Jamie's interference in a family matter, their friendship had grown to the point where they met up for a drink most weeks when he wasn't on the road.

It was at one of their regular get-togethers with the two of them and another couple of mates that the conversation had turned to matters of faith. Once again Ollie had let loose on his contempt for the duplicity of religious believers, and once again Jamie had sat patiently until the storm subsided. When things had gone quiet, he'd made the observation that whatever you thought of His present-day followers, Jesus remained a fascinating figure, and asked the question as to how tough it must be for anyone who tried to take his life and teaching seriously.

Ray was hanging on every word, wondering where all this was going to lead, when they were interrupted by Jamie's reappearance, bringing their breakfast. Reluctantly he agreed to wait for the conclusion of the story until they'd done justice to the fare that had been set before them. Between mouthfuls of food they exchanged pleasantries and their conversation felt more natural to Ray than any he could remember for a long time. That in itself, he reflected, would have made the 400-mile round trip worth it. For all that, he was glad when they pushed their plates aside, poured another cup of tea, and Ollie could get on with his story.

'To this day,' he said with a baffled expression, 'I'm not sure how we got there. Maybe we just had one drink too many. But we talked about what Jamie had said and, by the end of the night, the four of us had agreed to meet every Wednesday evening and go through one of the Gospels bit by bit and see what we could make of Jesus. It was my suggestion that we should read Mark's Gospel, just because I remembered that was the shortest one and I wasn't sure how long we'd stick with it. And I had the sense to make sure we used a modern translation.'

Ray was intrigued and surprised. Ollie had never fitted into the youth ministry at church. Now it seemed he was part of a Bible-study group! It was the last thing he'd expected to hear. He was barely able to contain his curiosity.

'So what happened?'

'Well, it was tough going at first. Jamie had done RE at school, so he had some familiarity with the stuff. Rob and Alan, the other two, are bright guys, both graduates. But neither of them really had anything more than the vaguest idea of the story. We got into some heated arguments about the miracles and we could've got bogged down in that. So we agreed to take it all at face value and just focus on what Jesus did and what he said and the people he met.'

Ollie paused to pour himself another cup of tea and Ray's face must have betrayed his disbelief at what he was hearing.

'I know,' Ollie laughed. 'I can hardly believe it myself. But here's the thing that really caught me out, took me by surprise. Jamie, knowing about our difficulties, quickly cast me in the role of the prodigal son – even before we got to that bit. It became a running joke. Nearly every time we met he'd pretend he was a continuity announcer introducing the next episode of a TV soap, and say in the deepest voice he could manage, "Is this the week Ollie starts the long walk home to his dad?" What actually happened was quite different…'

He took a long pause and gave a deep sigh, and Ray sensed that this wasn't a moment to interrupt or to try to fill the silence. When Ollie was ready to speak again, he pulled his chair closer and talked quietly and slowly. He was about to make a speech that he'd rehearsed in his mind a dozen times in preparation for this moment, but it still wasn't easy to say the words aloud.

'What happened was that I began to see myself, not as the prodigal son or one of the people that Jesus healed or fed or whatever, but as one of the Pharisees! I know that sounds crazy – me as one of the religious crowd. But here's the thing. I realised how self-righteous I've been. I've been condemning you and calling you a hypocrite. But you've at least attempted to take the Jesus stuff seriously. And you've done it for a long time. OK, you messed up, but you've obviously been distraught about all that's happened. And you've tried to say sorry to me more than once. And me? I've only lived half as long as you but I'm pretty sure my list of sins is a whole lot longer than yours. But I've been so convinced that I'm in the right and that I can tell you how to live, that I wouldn't even listen to your apology.'

Ray tried to interject at this point, but Ollie stopped him. He had one more thing he needed to say.

'Naah… let me finish, Dad. The point of telling you all this is that I'm trying to say that I forgive you and I want to apologise to you and ask for your forgiveness.'

Ray sat stock-still, trying to take it all in. Then he pushed his chair back and stood up.

'Come here, Ollie,' he said.

A lifetime of deeply ingrained Scottish reluctance to engage in any public show of emotion drained away as he reached out and pulled his son towards him. And years of resentment dissolved as Ollie threw his arms round his father. There was nothing more that needed to be said at that moment.

They might have stayed locked in that embrace much longer than they did, had they not suddenly become aware of the presence of a young woman with distinctive copper-coloured hair standing alongside them.

'Oh my,' she said, shaking her head. 'Fancy seeing you two stubborn men like this.'

'Ellen, where on earth did you come from?' Ollie asked in amazement.

'Well, if you'll sit down,' she said, moving Ray's coat and taking her place on the spare chair, 'I'll tell you.'

The explanation for her sudden and unexpected appearance was brief and simple. Knowing of Ollie's intention to set things right with his father, and fearing that he might lose his nerve at the last minute, she'd decided to make her way to Prince Charlie's Tipple – 'just in case you needed some encouragement'. She'd got there ten minutes or so prior to Ollie's arrival and found a place by the bar from where she thought she could watch the action without being seen. Her plan had worked perfectly and, having witnessed the encounter reach its more than satisfactory conclusion, she couldn't contain her joy a minute longer. The revelation of her ploy served only to add to the sense of elation.

Soon, despite the early hour, the cups and plates had been pushed aside and the three of them were standing to toast the success of the morning's meeting and the healing of a family's wounds. Ollie persuaded his dad to raise a glass of the amber liquid for which his native land was famed. Ellen, having ordered a fresh pot of Earl Grey tea, saw no reason to change from her favourite beverage, and was more than happy to clink her cup against their whisky glasses. Jamie, smiling broadly, put the tray he was carrying down on the bar, walked across the room and shook hands with them. Even the customers sitting at nearby tables, though they didn't know the full story, could see that there was cause for celebration and burst into a round of spontaneous applause. Ollie, who saw himself more as a self-righteous Pharisee recognising his failings rather than a prodigal son returning home, nonetheless couldn't help remembering the story in Luke's Gospel. And though he quickly dismissed the thought as fanciful and sentimental, probably brought on by drinking whisky too early in the day, for one fleeting moment he imagined he could hear the angels in heaven rejoicing over a sinner who had repented.

# Twenty

## A Wind of Change

They'd been in no hurry to leave Prince Charlie's Tipple and the one o'clock gun boomed out from the castle, startling them just as they stepped back out on to the street. The gloomy weather had begun to lift a little and the three of them ambled slowly down the Royal Mile. The temperature had increased only a degree or so, but the sky was clearing and a wintry sunshine had broken through. Ray was content just to walk alongside Ellen and Ollie, observing how comfortable they were in each other's company and listening to their easy conversation. They went with him as far as Princes Street where they parted under the shadow of the Scott Monument. For a full minute he stood and watched them walking away from him hand in hand until they disappeared from view in the crowd. It brought a pang of envy and regret as he remembered carefree days before his own marriage when he and Jean would stroll in similar fashion, unconcerned about the future, simply savouring the pleasure of being together. Alas, envy and regret, he now knew all too well, were wasted emotions that served only to deepen the sense of loss that was always just under the surface these days. He turned abruptly and made his way to his car.

He drove out of the city and headed south, following the same route that he'd taken almost two years earlier, until he joined the M6 motorway. On what seemed to him like a mere whim, he pulled in to the Tebay services. As soon as he'd settled himself at a table with a cup of coffee, however, he knew immediately that there was more to his apparently impulsive decision than he'd at first supposed. This, of course, was the place where he'd stopped on his way home from his previous ill-fated meeting with Ollie, where he'd sat and replayed the events that had brought about their bitter confrontation, where he'd resolved to tell Jean about his affair with Annie Chaplin, and where he'd set off from only to face the devastating news of Jean's death. And this, he now realised, was where he needed to summon his resolve and set his course for the future. What was done could never be undone, mistakes that he'd made could never be unmade, and life could never return to what it had once been. He'd messed things up, that couldn't be denied. And his faith was certainly not the clear and definite thing it had once been, that was beyond question. Within him, however – and to his surprise – there was a stirring of hope, faint and ill-defined as yet, like a vulnerable seedling struggling to push its way through the darkness of the earth and into the light of a sun that it had never seen.

Too much had happened to allow him to dismiss the story of his life as consisting only of betrayal and tragedy. And too many people had played a significant role for it to be merely about him and his faults and weaknesses. He thought of the cast of characters whose presence had not only kept him from what might have been the consequences of his despair and guilt, but had also helped to bring about a restoration of his relationship with his son: the loyal friendship of Tim and Carol; the practical concern of Eric Bradley in pulling him from the sea; the simple human kindness of the waitress in the tea room in Beaulieu; the robust counsel of Sam Andrews; the inspiration of Laura Sheldrick bringing beauty from brokenness; the zest for life that flowed from Ellen and that had done so much to change his son; the care that Charlie and Agnes had shown to the couple; the courage of Ollie's mate Jamie in challenging three young men against all the odds to take a look at the story of Jesus – these were all part of the drama of his life. That wasn't to deny that his failings were intrinsic to the plot, irrevocably written into the script. But they were not the whole story. His life – the good *and* the bad – was part of something bigger than himself, something more hopeful, something nobler. It was, he was beginning to sense, a drama being played out on a larger stage, against a bigger backdrop, and with a greater purpose. Of course, that was a truth he'd acknowledged and even taught to others as a Christian minister. But only now, as he was slowly emerging from the heartbreak and failure of the last couple of years, had it become something he felt in the depth of his being rather than just known as an article of faith to which he gave intellectual assent.

Dusk was falling as he walked back to his car and a cold breeze was whipping up the leaves that were scattered across the car park. The rooks that seemed to haunt that place every time he stopped there were circling and sweeping in the dying light of the day. He found the sight as hypnotically beautiful and captivating as ever, while, in contrast, the sound of their discordant cawing was as unsettling to him as it had always been. It threatened to cast him back into the kind of dark mood from which he'd only begun to escape in recent days until a sudden gust of wind seemed to scatter the birds, disturbing the pattern of their flight and momentarily drowning out the noise of their jarring calls. It was in itself an insignificant happening, an unremarkable combination of events in the natural world, nothing more than a flock of noisy birds blown a little off course by a sudden squall. But for Ray it was a moment of insight that took him deeper than cold logic and brought with it a hint of release from the fears that had haunted him since childhood.

The rooks that circled above him, moving him with the fluid beauty of their aerial choreography while simultaneously disturbing him with their repulsive cries, would for ever symbolise for him that perplexing tangle of good and evil that is shot through the fabric of the world. But for the first time it was as if he was observing the birds from the perspective of a greater reality; a force that could break in on them at any time, scatter them, lift them high or drop them low, and overpower the hideous clamour of their malevolent song. He knew in that instant that though the sight and sound of rooks at dusk would remain a disquieting image in his mind, they were not, and could not be, a window into the deeper truth of how things really were and how they would ultimately be.

There is a wind that blows where it will, untameable and unpredictable, often disrupting the established order of things, rearranging and reordering everything, and displaying an authority which every living being must acknowledge. Those who seek to resist it risk being destroyed. But those who abandon themselves to its power and ride the wind will find their strength renewed. They will learn new ways to live and to move through the world, bound to it and yet free, like eagles soaring in a clear blue sky.

He got into his car and sat quietly for several minutes, searching for a word or phrase to describe what had just happened, for a category in which to file it. Was it simply one of those odd experiences that happened from time to time, that seemed to be significant but turned out to be of no real consequence and were quickly forgotten? Or would it prove to be a moment of genuine epiphany, a moment in which he had glimpsed in his soul something of the truth at the heart of the universe? He'd had too many encounters with religious eccentrics in his life to be anything other than instinctively sceptical of people who make extravagant claims to mystical experiences, and he certainly had no desire to add himself to their number. For all that, he found himself making a conscious decision to accept it at face value, to receive it as an undeserved gift, and to trust the validity of what had just happened. After all, he reasoned, he'd nothing to lose. There was nothing else on which he could rely. He was alive thanks to the kindness of others, and his only hope was that their love and care was an echo of the reality that underpinned the entire created order. In his mind he could hear the voice of

Sam Andrews welcoming him to the 'Alliance of the Unworthy', and there and then, sitting in his car in a windswept motorway services, he decided it was time to enrol. He turned on the ignition and began the drive back to Manchester, fully recognising that there were major decisions to be faced in the days ahead, but at peace with himself and with the world.

Next morning he wasted no time in setting about the tasks that had to be done. Over breakfast he told Tim and Carol that he would start looking for alternative accommodation that day and be out their hair within the next couple of weeks. As he'd expected, they assured him that they were in no hurry to see him go, but he could sense that they were pleased that he was ready to step back into the stream of life. When they'd both left for the day, he stayed seated at the kitchen table with his laptop for an hour, putting together a CV and making a list of any advertised jobs that might suit his experience and abilities. He reckoned he'd just about enough remaining in his savings to tide him over for another few months so that he wouldn't need to claim statutory benefits. But, just in case that became necessary, he bookmarked the JobCentre website and noted the details of the local office. Even if he was unable to find a job that really suited him, he resolved to do whatever came up in order to begin earning a living again.

Only after all that did he address himself to the task he most wanted to do and yet most feared – sending an email to Annie Chaplin. He typed and deleted and retyped his message several times, struggling to find the right form of words. He tried to apologise for his long silence, to explain why he'd not been in touch and his reasons for contacting her now. But it all seemed so trite and unconvincing when he looked at the words on the screen in front of him. He would have given up and left it for another day had he not feared that he might cop out completely. In the end he settled for one brief sentence – one that came straight to the point:

Annie, can we meet please? Ray.

Before he could change his mind he hit the send button. Having avoided any contact with Annie for over a year, he'd no idea how she would respond or whether she'd even reply. For all he knew she might have met or even married someone else. He might be guilty of breaking in on her life and dredging up memories that she desperately wanted to forget. He was still rehearsing these unpalatable possibilities in his mind when he glanced back at the screen and saw that Annie had replied. She must have done so immediately she'd received his message, and that served only to throw him further into confusion. Did her quick response imply a positive reaction? Or did it mean a swift rejection of his request? It was a full five minutes before he could bring himself to open her email. As he clicked the mouse over the inbox, he noticed that his hand was shaking and his heart was pounding, and he realised just how important her reply was to him.

Ray, I'd love to meet. I'm at the Trafford Centre today recording some interviews for a programme. I'll be through by 2.30. Could meet at the coffee shop in the Great Hall. Shouldn't be too busy and we can find a table where we can talk without being overheard. So glad to hear from you. Annie.

It was more than he could have hoped for. He breathed a sigh of relief, logged out of his computer, and went for a five-mile run to fill in the time before their meeting.

It was exactly thirty-one minutes after two o'clock when Ray pushed open one of the heavy glass doors and walked into the Great Hall at the Trafford Centre. He'd been sitting in his car for twenty minutes, unsure whether he was summoning up his courage or merely whiling away the time to avoid arriving early and looking overeager. Now he was worried about being late! As he entered, he glanced up at the enormous ornate chandelier – it always reminded him of a drawing Ollie had made of a spaceship when he was just starting school – suspended above the sweeping staircase with its grandiose marble balustrade that led ostentatiously to the upper level of this temple to consumerism. The strangely eclectic combination of rococo and neo-classical styles with a bit of art deco thrown in for good measure always had the effect of making him think he'd arrived in some kind of parallel universe in which the norms of good judgement and common sense no longer prevailed. Today, ironically, it felt like just the right setting. Two years ago, if someone had predicted to him the meeting that was about to take place and the proposal he was about to make, he'd either have laughed out loud or been quietly horrified at such an implausible suggestion. Now, like the architecture and décor of this place, it had a logic all of its own. It seemed right for this place and time.

He looked across to the coffee shop on his left, scanning the tables for where Annie might be sitting. She wasn't there and his first thought was that she'd changed her mind. Then he saw her – walking down the stairs, casually dressed with a leather bag slung over her shoulder, obviously still in work mode. As soon as she saw him her face broke into a smile and she hurried towards him.

'Ray Young,' she said, kissing him on the cheek. 'It's good to see you. You're looking trim and fit. Your travels must have done you good.'

He suddenly felt awkward and clumsy, just like he'd done when they'd met for the first time at the BBC studios. At least this time, he thought to himself, he didn't have the added disadvantage of wet hair and damp clothes.

'Well, I hope they did,' he replied returning her greeting. 'I'm certainly older and I hope a little bit wiser. And you look…' he struggled for the right words, worried about saying the wrong thing and getting their meeting off to a bad start. '…well, you look just like you.'

Annie said she wasn't sure if that was good or bad, but that she'd take it as a compliment any way. They both laughed which helped to ease the tension.

They ordered their coffee and carried it to a table tucked behind a pillar which afforded them the privacy they needed. For the first few minutes they contented themselves with small talk until Annie's curiosity and impatience got the better of her.

'Ray, I really want to know what's been happening to you since I last saw you. When we met before Jean's funeral I could see that you needed to get away by yourself for a while. And I've respected that and haven't tried to get in touch. But it's been tough. I've thought about you every day. It feels like you owe me some kind of explanation.'

'How long have we got?' he asked.

'As long as it takes.'

Annie's reply was good-natured but firm. And it was clear to him that she wasn't going to be put off.

Ray pushed his cup away, pulled his chair closer, put his elbows on the table, intertwined his fingers, rested his chin on the backs of his hands, and cleared his throat. It was, as Ollie had noted many months before in an Edinburgh hostelry, the routine to which he always defaulted when he had something of significance to say. He began to tell her the long saga of the journey he'd taken since their last meeting.

It took almost two hours and another couple of refills of their cups before he'd reached the end of his story. Annie listened intently, never interrupting and barely even moving. When he'd finished and pushed his chair back she shook her head slowly. Her voice wavered a little and her usual confidence seemed to have deserted her.

'Well… you've been on a life-changing odyssey and I've been doing the same old stuff every day. Do you know what you're going to do now?'

Her face had an expression of utter desolation, like someone who has been abandoned and left alone in some dreary and deserted place. Ray knew that this was the moment to tell her where his journey had led him to.

'Yes, I do know what I'm going to do. Or at least, I know what I *want* to do. But that depends on you as much as me.'

He reached across the table and touched her hand for just a moment.

He glanced around to check that they were not being overheard by anyone, before he went on. His voice was quiet but clear and purposeful.

'Just seeing you again is enough to make me realise that my feelings for you are still very strong. But I can never get away from the fact that what we did was wrong and nothing we can do or say can ever make that right. So there's no way we can just pick up from where we left off.'

He could see the tears begin to well up in her eyes and he felt his resolve weaken. But he knew that for the sake of them both he needed to get to the end of what he had to say.

'I wronged my wife, and I wronged you, too. I know we're both adults and we're *both* responsible for what happened. But I was the married man. I was the respected Christian speaker. The onus was on me to stop things before they got too far. So I want to do things right now. And I want to do right by you. Let me tell you where I'm at.'

He paused and took a moment trying to put the words he'd been rehearsing in his mind all morning into some proper order.

'The first thing I need to do now is to get back into normal life, find myself a job, decide where I'm going to live – practical stuff like that. The truth is, we both need to draw a line under the past and make a new start. Let's take six months before we think of even meeting again. See how things look then, how we feel about each other, about everything. It may well be – it probably is – best for us to go our separate ways. And I know it wouldn't be right for us just to move in with each other. I know it sounds ridiculously old-fashioned after all that's happened and impossibly romantic for a man of my age. But if by any chance we do have a future together, I want us to have a proper courtship, to meet each other like we're doing now, to go out on dates, to have arguments with each other and make up again. You know, all the usual messy stuff that couples do when they're getting to know each other. And only if we're both sure that we're ready and we can deal with the past, let's talk about the future, what that might mean for us, how it might impact others...'

He was aware of the sound of his own voice using words and phrases that were unfamiliar, so unlike his usual conversation, and his courage began to drain away. What if someone could overhear him? Worse still, what if Annie reacted badly and there was an unpleasant scene? Any pretence of eloquence deserted him and he was suddenly tongue-tied, unsure how to finish his sentence. To his relief, Annie simply smiled through her tears and began to gather up her things as she spoke.

'Ray, I couldn't ask you for anything more. Don't spoil it by saying anything else. It's been good to see you today. And I'm willing to wait and see what the future brings. Now, be a gentleman and walk me to my car. I've got to get back to the studio.'

They walked out to the car park together. It was already dark, and in the cold evening air, their first instinct was to draw just a little closer together for warmth. But it was one they both resisted. As they parted and said goodbye, they both knew that something significant had just happened. It had been a moment of honesty and healing, perhaps even one of hope.

That night Ray could not sleep. He sat in his bedroom until the small hours pondering the past and wondering what the future might bring. The temperature had continued to drop, and though it could only have been a degree or so above freezing, he pulled a chair over to the window, opened it wide, and took deep breaths of the cold air. He was overcome with a sense of gratitude for life. He could not mend what had been broken or undo what had been done. But he could set a new course. He reached over to the bookshelf and took down the leather-bound book with which he'd been so familiar but which he'd neglected for what seemed such a long time. He would start in the same place as Ollie had done and see what it might say to *him* about who *he* was and what *he* needed to do. As he opened the book at the start of Mark's Gospel, a sudden breeze from the open window wafted the pages. It stirred a memory somewhere deep within him and he smiled to himself. He held the fluttering pages in place and began to read softly and slowly:

The beginning of the good news about Jesus...[2]

---

[2] Mark 1:1 (NIV UK 2011).